A Nothing and a Nobody

By

Joyce Dicus

This book is a work of fiction. Places, events, and situations in this story are purely fictional. Any resemblance to actual persons, living or dead, is coincidental.

ISBN: 1-4033-8176-3 (e-book)
ISBN: 1-4033-8177-1 (Paperback)

This book is printed on acid free paper.

1stBooks - rev. 01/09/03

Table of Contents

Prolog

It was the 1960's. In leaps and bounds the world was changing. These changes, however, had not yet touched the lives of the people who lived in the hills of rural Tennessee near a place called Flatwoods. Jain was one of these people. She came from a very poor family. They lived in a house that the family had built themselves, with the only tools that they owned, a chopping ax, a crosscut saw, and a buck saw. The rafters of the house were the long, tall pine trees that grew near-by. Her dad had patiently taught his children as they all worked together to build the house. They had put the small end of the trees to the top so that there wouldn't be too much weight and cause the house to fall. Her mother, without cracking a smile, had told the kids that if they bent a nail, it meant that they didn't love her. It was her way of keeping them from wasting the nails. When completed, the house looked shabby, but it would stand there on the hillside long after the family had moved away. They had no way of knowing that their dad would be dead, just a precious memory that would remain with them forever by the time he was fifty years old. Other memories of that life would also remain, some of them good, in spite of the hardships that they endured, others would leave them scared forever.

They still had wood heat and kerosene lamps, while most of the world around them had electricity. Houses were nestled deep in the woods, miles apart, some not even visible from the road. In the wintertime, you could see the spirals of smoke rising from the tops of the houses and disappearing over the tops of the trees into the clouds. Their dad would chop the trees that they used for wood down before he went to work, because he didn't want a tree to fall on the children and hurt them. Jain and her brother pulled the old cross cut saw and cut them into sticks. Getting wood for the cook stove was easier. They just took the chopping ax into the woods and got the dead dogwood and dead sour wood trees that her mother liked best for cooking, dragged them back to the yard and used the chop block to cut them into small sticks for the cooking stove. Sometimes, they took time to cut a grapevine and swing out from the hillside or across a gully on it. They carried drinking water from a spring in five-gallon buckets. They raised their own food, grew their own vegetables, and killed their own chickens for Sunday dinner. If visitors dropped by unexpectedly, they ate first and the children ate last, according to family custom. There was one uncle that would eat the whole bowl of fried potatoes and all of the biscuits before leaving the table. Jain and the other kids dreaded to see him coming, for hunger was no stranger to this family.

Being the oldest child, Jain was adept at using a hoe, a chopping ax, and at killing the chickens. She cried each time that she had to grab a chicken by the neck and wring its head from its body. She could feel the bone snap in her hand. Seeing the body flopping around on the ground without its head made her cringe inside. When the chicken stopped flopping around, she would pluck the feathers from it's body, then singe the fine feathers from it by lighting a match and sticking it to a twisted, brown paper bag. She ran the flame over the entire chicken, then it was washed, gutted, and cut into pieces. Her mother fried it a crisp, golden brown for Sunday dinner and served it with a big bowl of gravy and a big pan of hot biscuits. Food was a treat. Often, there wasn't really enough for a large family of eight. They knew how it felt to be hungry and cold. It was a way of life.

Food was more plentiful and they ate better in the summertime when the fresh vegetables from the garden were in season. The corn that had been "laid-by", the term that they used to describe the final hoeing and weeding, at least five times was delicious. Add a red, ripe tomato, a few green onions and a piece if corn bread and it was the best meal in the world.

Jain's, childhood had been neither easy nor happy. It wasn't that she didn't love her family, because she did. She had just never felt that she belonged or fit into it. She always felt like a fish out of water, like no one really knew her. She cried a lot. Her Dad understood her better than anyone else, but even he would say,

"Oh, that's just Jain. She was born a crying and she'll die a crying." She knew that she was a big disappointment to her family, that she wasn't really what they wanted her to be. She often wished that she were dead or that she had never been born. Once, she had taken a whole bottle of aspirin and tried to kill herself, but it didn't work. She survived and no one even knew the difference. She grew up in spite of everything. In her world, the only way for a girl to change her circumstances was marriage and she daydreamed of this.

Now her dreams were coming true! She was getting married! She was bursting with happiness. Her heart was overflowing with love. She stood before the preacher in her white cotton dress, and vowed to God and everybody, to love that man until her dying day. Visions of living happily ever after filled her head. She was eager to leave her childhood behind. She believed that her family would be happy to see her married and settled. It would be one less mouth to feed and times were hard. She knew that they had feared that Jain would be "an old maid." It was their custom for a girl to be married at age eighteen, if not, they were labeled an old maid.

Ten years and two children later, it all fell apart. Ray, the man that she had built her life around, had left her for a teenage girl. At age thirty, she thought her life had ended. Her heart was broken; her life was shattered. She completely fell apart.

Feelings of shame engulfed her. She couldn't hold her head up. She was a failure. The hurt! Oh God, how she hurt. She couldn't eat. She couldn't sleep. It took every ounce of her energy just to care for the kids and go to work. Once again, she wanted to die.

It was more than just loosing the man, even though she'd loved him more than she loved her own life. It was knowing that her children wouldn't have their father around. It was knowing that she was a failure. It was not being able to live up to the Holy vows that she had made before God. No one seemed to understand that. She thought about the verse in the Bible, where it said that if a man put away his wife, he caused her to commit adultery. Was she now an adulteress? She felt like she'd lost half of herself.

How could he do this? Why? What did I do wrong? How could I have not known? Why can't I fix it? Why didn't I see it comming? What will I do without him? Oh God, how can I go on? These were some of the thoughts that ran constantly through her head.

She would go on, though, because she had no other choice. Two wide - eyed, frightened children stood looking up at her. Their world had also been shattered. She silently promised that she would always be there for them.

chapter 1

Thank God it's Saturday, thought Jain. She had worked all week at the local garment factory as a machine operator. She set back pockets on men's pants, eight hours a day, five days a week, and made just a little over minimum wage. Often, as now, it was the sole source of income for the family. Her husband, Ray, had quit his job three weeks ago, and still hadn't found another one. This was nothing new. He seldom held a job for more than three months at a time. When he was employed, she had to beg him to get up and go to work. He liked to sleep 'till ten, then cruise the streets all day. He was often late when he picked Jain up from work. If she asked where he had been, he'd just get mad. The folks at work had a name for men like Ray. They called them real go-getters. They said,

"She goes to work and he goes and gets her." It used to make Jain mad.

As she was doing the breakfast dishes, Ray called out, "I'll be back after while." The front door slammed, and she heard him gun the motor. Gravel flew as he peeled out of the driveway, in the souped up chevy with glass packs, that was his pride and joy. He was not lazy when it came to that car. He kept it waxed and shinning.

Jain sighed. She could have used a little help with the chores and the kids. Her heart melted when she looked at the children. They were her pride and joy, her reason for living. Just being with them made all the bad times worthwhile. "Thank you, Lord," she breathed. Anger and disappointment fled before they could take root.

Six-year old Cassity was sitting in the floor, playing with her Barbie doll. Cass had long, straight brown hair with blond highlights that she got from her mom, and big beautiful blue eyes that came from her dad. She looked up at her mom and asked, "Is Daddy comming back? Can we still go to town?"

"Yeah," Jain sat on the floor and started to play with the children. "He'll be back by the time we get the house clean and get you ready. What do you want to buy today?" They shopped for groceries every Saturday. It was a family outing.

"Hot dogs!" piped Stanley. He looked even more like Ray than Cassity did, with his wavy brown hair, so dark that it was almost black. He was busy taking his toy truck apart. He was better at taking things apart than he was at putting them back together. Last week, he took the alarm clock apart and it still didn't work right. There was no money to buy another one. Jain was afraid she'd oversleep and be late for work.

"That's what he always wants!" Cass was not too impressed with her eighteen-month-old brother. "Mom, can we make Barbie a new dress?"

Stanley stuck the cat under his arm, head down, tail up, and headed toward the bathroom. Jain went to rescue the cat. There was a knock on the door, and in walked Ray's mother, Lydia.

"Can you wash and set my hair today?" This was an almost weekly routine, but Jain kind of enjoyed it. She wanted to be closer to her mother-in-law. The sense of not belonging that had plagued her all her life had carried over into Ray's family. She still felt like an outsider. She still craved a feeling that she belonged.

Jain put the cat out and turned on the television for the kids, glad to have another grown up to talk to. She needed to tell someone about her worries, to talk about her problems, but sharing her truest feelings didn't come easy. If she complained to her friends at work about Ray, they would just say; "Why don't you leave him?" Her relationship with her mother in law wasn't all that great, but she kept hoping that it would get better. Jain tried really hard. She had even taught Lydia how to drive.

Now, as she put the last roller in place and secured it with a bobbypin, she said; "I sure hope Ray finds a job soon. All the bills are about a month behind and Cass needs school cloths. I can't believe she's old enough to go to school."

Two red splotches of color appeared on Lydia's face. Her jaws puffed out. Jain could feel her bristle. "Let me tell you something right now, poor little Ray is not able to work!" As she spoke, she turned around and pointed her finger in Jain's face for emphasis. "You of all people should know that."

Shocked, Jain swallowed an angry retort and turned on the hair dryer. 'Poor little Ray' stood six feet and two inches tall and weighed two hundred and thirty eight pounds. He was in the National Guard Reserves. He had joined the National Guard to keep from getting drafted and having to go Viet Nam. Jain was five feet and two inches tall, and her weight was one hundred and twenty pounds. Conversation was a little strained after that, and Lydia left as soon as her hair was done. Jain finished her chores, then spent time with the children. She was determined to enjoy her weekend. She hoped that Lydia didn't run into Ray. When there was a disagreement, he always sided with his mother.

By the time Ray returned the house was fairly clean, and Barbie had several new outfits. The cat looked a little ragged, but was unharmed, and Stanley had taken two toy trucks apart. They made it to the store with time to spare, and even went by the drive-thru restaurant for hamburgers. The children giggled in the back seat and Jain realized that she was happy with her life in spite of everything.

"I may have a job," Ray told her as she put away the groceries. "The whole town is talking about all the city cops walking off the job. They got mad at the mayor. He wouldn't approve a pay raise. The chief says that if they don't come back to work by Monday, he will replace them all. He says that being in the Guard will help me get a job."

"I was hoping that you'd get a job, but isn't that dangerous?"

"In this little hick town? How can you be so stupid? It's all just politics. You just have to know who to arrest and who to leave alone."

Ray got the job, working the three to eleven shift and he really seemed to like it. It was the first time in the ten years of their marriage that Jain didn't have to beg him to go to work. He looked so handsome in his uniform. He was proud and confident as he patrolled the streets in the police cruiser. He even paid some of the bills. Jain's hopes soared. She thought about getting her G.E.D. and getting a better job. Ray didn't want her to do that. He thought that she should keep working at the factory.

Everywhere that she went, she heard people talking about the new cop. The women thought he was good looking. The men said that he thought he was smart and that he needed to be brought down a notch or two.

The family said that he was letting the uniform go to his head. Jain knew what they meant, she could feel him changing, feel him slipping further away, but she was powerless to stop it.

They were drifting further and further apart. Ray no longer wanted to be seen in public with her and the children. He now found excuses to go places alone. He didn't want to visit family or friends, but he still came home for supper every night. He made it clear that he expected Jain to be there. If she ran out of milk and went to the store, he accused her of "running around, spending his money, and checking up on him." Jain was bewildered. People at work were talking about Ray and giving her strange looks.

The gossip around town grew worse. She now heard things like; "He thinks he's God's gift to women." Or; "He's going to get what he deserves one of these days. Someone is going to teach him a lesson." People continued to give her strange looks when she went out in public. She even got strange stares at the grocery store. She could tell that some people felt sorry for her, and she hated pity. She could feel her world falling apart but she didn't know how to stop it from happening.

When Jain told Ray what the people were saying, and how they were acting, he just thought it was funny.

"They're just jealous, just a bunch of losers. You shouldn't be listening to them."

Still, Jain couldn't shake her feelings of gloom and apprehension. Ray came home later each night. She started waiting up for him, even though she had to get up at five am in order to get Stan to the baby sitter, Cass ready for school, and be at work by seven. When

Jain asked why he was late, or where he had been, it made him furious.

"Where were you?" she asked one night when he was over an hour late. "I was getting worried. I was afraid that something had happened to you." His reaction stunned her. She had waited up for him and had been walking toward him, but now she stood frozen in her tracks.

Ray clenched his fists and his face drained of color. He looked like he wanted to murder her. "Why don't you leave me alone?" he ranted "It's none of your business where I go or what I do! You're not my keeper." He stomped off to bed, leaving her in tears.

Things got worse with each passing week. She learned to avoid the late night fights. She still waited up, but now she paced the floor in the dark. When she heard the car pull into the drive, she hurried to bed and pretended to be asleep. The gulf between them grew wider. It was like living with a stranger. Jain felt like Ray was leaving her behind, cutting her out of his life, and she was powerless to stop it, yet that's what she wanted so desperately to do. Ray and the kids were her reason for living.

Once a year, the carnival came to town. It was a big event and almost everyone went. The kids especially loved it. Ray was assigned to patrol the fair grounds, for along with the carnival, came increased crimes, mostly pick pockets and thefts. Tuesday was half-price night. On Monday, when Ray came home for supper, Jain said, "I think I'll take the kids to the fair tomorrow night. It's the cheap night." She smiled, thinking of running into kinfolk's that she hadn't seen in a year. Folks from all the surrounding counties would be there. There would be miniature family reunions.

All the air suddenly left the room. Ray slammed his fist onto the table, making the plates bounce. "You will do no such thing!" he shouted. "Especially not tomorrow night. How do you think that would look, with my wife over there spying on me?"

"Spying on you?" Jain was in shock. "Spying on you - - What are you talking about? I just wanted to take the kids to the fair. I've been saving the money for three weeks. Cass is looking forward to it. Her friend Tracie is going. Stan will wear me out, but it will be worth it. He's big enough to ride the kiddy rides. They'll have so much fun."

"I mean it Jain, you had better not go over there. It wouldn't look right for you to be out running around while I'm at work."

"Oh for goodness sake, Ray. I was only going to take them for an hour or so. We could go after supper and be home before ten. They could ride the rides and get cotton candy. That's all they care about doing anyway."

She loved him. He had to know that. Cheating on him or doing him wrong in any way had never crossed her mind. She thought it over and convinced herself that she might feel the same way, if she were in his place. Still, it was a shame that Cass couldn't go. Stan would probably get cranky and tired, but Cass was just the right age to enjoy a little carnival like that. She couldn't justify making Cass miss the fun. Maybe some of the family was going and would come by and take her. Please, Lord, she prayed silently, don't let Cass have to miss the carnival. She wanted her children to have a happy childhood. She wanted their lives to be happier than hers.

Her prayer was answered. Tuesday evening, Dave and Ruth came by. Dave was only thirteen years old when Jain and Ray got married. Now he and Ruth were thinking about marriage. Dave was Ray's baby brother, but he and Jain had always had a special bond. He seemed almost like one of her children, and Ruth had seemed like family since the first time that Jain met her. They usually stopped by once or twice a week. Cass worshipped Dave.

"Hey, Brat!" Dave caught Cass up in the air as she made a leap for him. "We're headed to the fair," he said to Jain. "You and the kids want to tag along?"

"I want to go! I want to go! Can we Mom?" Cass was jumping all around.

Jain hesitated. She didn't want to disappoint Cass, but she didn't want to make Ray mad again. She told Dave and Ruth about the way Ray felt, and how bad she felt about disappointing her daughter.

"We could take Cass." Ruth volunteered. Dave was quick to agree. He enjoyed impressing Ruth by showing her how good he was with kids, but it wasn't just an act. Jain knew that he really loved the kids. She told Cass to get a jacket and to be a good girl. An hour later, they were back, and Jain could tell that something was very wrong. Ruth stayed in the car, while Dave brought Cass into the house. He wouldn't look Jain in the eye, just kept looking down at his feet. He acted like he didn't know what to say. This was unreal. She had never seen Dave act this way. Cass was too quiet as well. Her bottom lip was stuck out, a sure sign that something was wrong in her world. Jain wondered if Dave and Ruth were arguing. They seemed happy enough earlier.

"What's wrong? Did the rides make her sick? Was it a bad idea to take her on your date?" Jain's concern was making her nervous. She was babbling.

"No, she's fine. She was good, we just had to leave early." Dave was already backing out the door, still looking at his feet. "See you later." He almost ran to the car.

With her head hung down and her bottom lip still stuck out, Cass kicked a toy across the floor. "Daddy was at the fair. He won Roni a teddy bear. I wanted one, but he said no. He made Dave bring me home. I didn't even get to ride the Ferris Wheel. Daddy was mad and said Dave should mind his own business." She went into her room and closed the door, leaving Jain with unanswered questions. She needed answers.

Ray had some explaining to do when he got home. She paced as she waited. Sleep was out of the question. Cass had refused comfort and cried herself to sleep. Jain was mad.

Ray was two hours late getting home. Anxious, puzzled, and angry, Jain met him at the door. She was too angry to be worried about him tonight. Her green eyes were bright with unshed tears, and the light reflecting in them made them sparkle. With her hands on her hips and her straight brown hair falling about her shoulders, she looked him in the eye. "Where have you been, and who is Roni? Did Cass see you with someone else at the fair? Is that why you didn't want me to take the kids tonight? Are you cheating on me?"

"None of your business! Cass overreacted. You've got those kids so spoiled." Jain could feel the hatred comming from him. "I told you to keep the kids home!

Get it through your head once and for all! Where I go and what I do is none of your business. You are a nothing Jain! A nothing and a nobody! Do you hear me? I'm not like you, I have friends. If you would mind your own business and stay home and tend to the kids like you are supposed to, there would be no problem." He hit the wall so hard with his fist that it left a hole in the sheetrock. "That was low, Jain, sending my brother and my child to spy on me like that!"

The fight that night woke the kids and made them cry. By the time Jain got them to calm down and go back to sleep, Ray was also asleep. He was snoring. There was no sleep for Jain that night. Ray was cheating on her. She had to face it now. She felt as stupid as he was always saying she was. Friends had tried to tell her, but she wouldn't take the hints seriously. She remembered getting mad at her friend, Livie, for telling her that Ray had a girlfriend. Their friendship was still strained. Ray and the children were her life. This could not be happening to her. What would she do if Ray left her? What would people say? On some level, she had known that Ray was cheating, still she had denied it. It really hurt. She wanted to strangle him. At the same time, she wanted to salvage her marriage. Some marriages survived affairs, maybe hers would.

She thought of how everyone talked about divorced women, how they put them down. She did not want a life like that for her children. There had to be a way to fix it. Even though it made her mad to think about it, she knew that she still loved Ray. She could not imagine a life without him. She went to work the next morning with dark circles under her eyes. Friends kept their distance and talk was subdued when she was in earshot. Jain withdrew more and more from her friends. Her world continued to fall apart.

Ray came home on time for the next three nights. They didn't mention the fair or Roni. The atmosphere was strained, but at least there were no more fights. Then Saturday came, and Ray had to work. He didn't come home at the usual time. When he was an hour late, Jain called the station and asked to speak to him. She didn't identify herself, and the dispatcher did not recognize her voice. She was told that Ray's shift had ended at eleven and he had gone home. It was a five-minute drive from home to work. By two am, he still wasn't home. She began to panic. She imagined him in a car wreck, or maybe someone had beaten him up and he was in the hospital, but when she called, he wasn't there. She had to do something. She bundled the kids into the car and started looking for him. She checked the parking lots, and all the backstreets and alleys, but there was no sign of him. Town looked dead. Finally, she gave up and went home. Thirty minutes later, he walked in, not a hair out of place, and happy as could be.

"Where were you? I called the station; they said you left at eleven. I looked everywhere for you. I thought you were hurt or dead or something." She reached for him. He shoved her away. "I told you to mind your own business. Leave me alone. You will get me fired if you call the station. I don't need you checking up on me."

That was the first hint that things were not so well with his job, but she buried her head a little deeper in the sand. She went on as usual, going to work, taking care of the children and home. She tried harder to keep him happy and avoid the fights. Later, she would wonder how anyone could ever be such a fool.

Soon after that, the dreams started. She prayed each night after she put the kids to bed. That's when she could really pour her heart out to God. She'd been praying for her marriage to last, for Ray to love her and the kids enough to end his affair with Roni. Now, she dreaded to go to sleep, no matter how tired she might be. It was the same dream every night, in living color. An eight by ten photo in a silver frame floated before her eyes. The woman was very young, a little on the plump side, with fair skin and blue eyes. She had long, straight blond hair. She didn't smile; in fact she showed no expression. The image floated before her until Jain would wake herself up, crying, "Ray, don't leave- - -"

One night, she awoke from the dream and was suddenly afraid. There was a commotion on the porch, then a knock on the door. Grabbing her robe, she raced to the window just in time to see a car drive away. When she opened the door, she saw a folded piece of paper in the mailbox. Frightened, she stuck the paper in her pocket and checked the house inside and out. The children slept peacefully, all the doors and windows were still locked, there was no one in the yard, but Jain was jumpy. Her nerves were shot. She had been sleep deprived for months. She sat down and pulled the paper from her pocket. She read it three times. She wanted to think it was a sick joke. If she had not been so hurt, it would have been funny. She read the large, childish scrawl again.

Dear Mrs. Davis,

I am in love with your husband. We have been going together for eleven weeks. He does not love you. You need to but out and let us be happy.

Roni

Deep down inside, Jain knew it was true. Ray wasn't just cheating on her. She was really loosing him. It wasn't just a one-time thing that happened during the fair, as she'd tried to convince herself for the past few days. He was really involved with someone else; still she had to ask him. She didn't bother going back to bed, and he came home on time that night. When she thrust the paper in his face, he wasn't even surprised.

"Get real, Jain. She's just a kid who has a crush on me. I'm friends with her parents. How dumb can you be?" He made it sound so simple.

It was a thin little straw, but she grasped it and held on for dear life.

A few days later, she got a letter through the regular mail. This one was from Roni's grandmother. It told her times, places, and details of Ray's meetings with Roni.

The grandmother made no bones about it; she wanted whatever Roni wanted. She asked what Jain was going to do about it. She enclosed a picture of Roni, smiling over Ray's shoulder, her arms around his neck. Jain recognized her as the girl she'd seen in her dreams every night. She felt a little more life seep out of her body.

By now, Ray had been a policeman for about four months. That was the longest that he'd ever held a job, but as Jain thought about the changes in their lives over the last four months, she wished that he had never gotten this job. Family and friends now avoided them. Even Lydia didn't come to get her hair done on Saturdays now. People at work looked at her like she was crazy. Some looked at her with pity her. Her self-esteem was at rock bottom. The children were less active and much too quiet. Things could not go on like this. When he came home for supper, she handed him the letter and the photo.

"This girl is not much older than your daughter! You could go to jail! How could you do this?"

She expected him to deny it, to blame her, or to laugh it off, but he just sat on the sofa and placed his head in his hands. "O. K. It's true. I love her. I didn't mean for it to happen, it just did. She's sixteen, almost seventeen. It's a mess. Her parents are mad at me. The chief says that I'd better get things straightened out soon or I won't have a job. I'm leaving you, Jain. I want a divorce. I'm going to marry her."

The next day, he packed his cloths and left as soon as he finished breakfast. Jain had no pride. She begged him not to go. He pushed her aside, then ignored her. He didn't even try to explain to the kids, didn't even tell them that he wouldn't be back.

Jain was in shock. She moved about like a zombie. She couldn't eat or sleep. She cried day and night. She didn't eat for three days. She lost twenty pounds that she didn't need to loose, and huge, dark circles appeared beneath her eyes. Her skin looked like it was stuck to her bones and turned a dull, gray shade. One morning, she got up and fixed breakfast as usual. She got the kids settled at the table and poured herself a glass of milk. She had no appetite, but she knew that she had to eat to keep going. She took a sip and swallowed. Her throat closed up and the milk stayed right there in her mouth. It wouldn't go down. She almost panicked. She tried again. Her throat was closed off. She tried three more times to swallow the milk before she gave up and spit it into the sink. At that point, she knew that she had to have help. She called in sick to work, then she asked her neighbor to watch the kids. Not knowing what else to do, she went to the doctor.

In this small town, everybody knew everybody. There were few, if any secrets that Dr. Andrews was not aware of. He was a kindly country doctor that took a real interest in his patients. He peeked his head into the waiting room, then spoke to his receptionist in a low voice that only she could hear. Humming a little tune, he went back down the hall.

. "Jain, you can go back now." Jain heard the sympathy in her voice, but perceived it as pity. She was embarrassed because she knew the entire staff by first name. She saw them at church and at the grocery store. She wished she could just hide from the world.

The nurse took her vital signs, smiled, patted her hand, and left the room, placing her chart in a slot outside the door. When the doctor walked in, the nurse started to follow, but he waved her away.

"Humm—-" He waited for Jain to make eye contact. He laid the chart on the table and sat on his rolling stool. "Tell me about it." He said about three more words, and Jain spilled her guts.

"I thought I could get through this by myself, but I can't. I can't even swallow milk." She talked for an hour, and he listened to every word. When she left, she had a prescription for valium, but already, the lump in her throat was going away. The prescription would never need a refill. She had found friends, as well as caring professionals. She took a pill that night and slept like a log. If the next day had not been a Saturday, she would have been late for work. She was able to eat breakfast with the children. She knew that she was going to make it. She had to for the children's sake.

They needed a car. Ray had taken theirs. She had been walking to work and to the grocery and getting a neighbor to watch the kids. This couldn't go on. She got her mom to co-sign a note at the bank and she bought a used Pontiac. It looked a little rough, but it was in good mechanical condition. It would work well for now.

She took the children for picnics in the park. Life began to seep slowly back into her and she even smiled a little these days. Money was tight, but she could get by. It didn't hurt as bad now, when she saw Ray drive through town with his arm around Roni. Just when things were getting better, work slowed down at the factory. There was talk that it might close. Her hours were cut back. Some people were laid off. She was lucky if she got to work three days a week. She had not seen one penny from Ray. After she paid the rent, the electric bill and the water, not to mention the car payment, there wasn't much money for food. There was an apple tree in her back yard, with plenty of apples. The children loved fried apple pies, and Jain cooked them almost daily. They would have fried apples and biscuits for breakfast and cooked apples, beans and bread for the other two meals. Fearing that the kids would be hungry or starve, Jain swallowed what was left of her pride, and went to the Dept. of Human Services. She signed up for food stamps and was assigned a caseworker. She was asked questions about child support, and everything else. She felt liked she had been beaten and pounded into the ground. She didn't know where to turn or what to do next.

The case worker visited her home, checked out her work situation, talked with her family and neighbors and even had Ray come in for an interview. Once she really knew the situation, she really helped. Ray signed 'Unable, Unwilling To Support' papers, and Jain and the kids qualified for food stamps, medicaid and aide for dependent children, That would help a lot, but it would not happen over night. The social worker told Jain how to apply for a pale grant, where and when to go and take her G.E.D., and slowly Jain began to venture into another way of life. The seed of hope had been replanted.

By now, Jain and the kids were used to doing without, but life continued to get worse. She was down to working two days a week. She qualified for help, but it would be weeks before she would get a check or food stamps. Her family couldn't help. She was desperate. Money and food dwindled. One morning, when she went to the kitchen to make breakfast, she discovered that she had only one cup of flour. She mixed it with water from the tap and made it into two biscuits. She fed one to Cass and one to Stan. Like the woman in the Bible, she thought they would eat it and die. All she could do was pray. She had never felt so hopeless in her life. There was nowhere to turn. She begged God to help. The next morning, she looked in the mailbox, expecting a bill, and found the food stamps. They came a full week early! To Jain, it was a miracle she wouldn't forget.

"Get ready!" she told the kids, "We're going to the store and you can buy anything that you want to eat!"

"Ice cream! I Want cake and ice cream," chanted Cass.

"Hot dogs!" Stanley dropped the cat and joined in, "I want hot dogs"

Jain started to laugh, but ended up sitting in the middle of the floor crying. She gathered her children into her arms and promised them that things would get better.

At the store, the children danced from isle to isle, filling the buggy with foods that they had not been able to afford for months. Jain didn't make them put anything back. She just couldn't. There were cokes, candy, cake, ice cream, potato chips, and hotdogs, along with the staples like milk, bread, eggs and vegetables. They passed by the meat counter, and Jain couldn't resist. She bought three small steaks. She was so hungry that her stomach rumbled and her mouth watered when she saw them.

At the check out counter, the kids were hanging onto the buggy like they thought the food was going to disappear. Two older ladies were in line behind them, dressed in suits and heels, make up on, and not a hair out of place. When Jain handed the food stamps to the cashier, she heard one of them say; "Just look how they waste our tax money on all that junk food."

"And steak!" her friend answered. "People who live on food stamps should know they can't afford steak."

Jain's face turned bright red, her spirit wilted, and she felt like she shrank an inch. She bit her lip and said nothing. She would not have this day spoiled for her children. Today, at least, they were going to have all the food that they wanted. She didn't care what anyone thought. She vowed that she would make them a better life. They would not always live like this. Anger began to grow along with determination inside her.

The next week, she took her G.E.D. test. A few weeks later, she got the results.

Her scores were high. She applied for the nursing class at the community college in the neighboring town. Now she waited to see if she would be accepted. She prayed harder than she ever had before. The factory closed, but she found a job as a waitress at Shoney's. The pay was pitiful, and she was too shy to get good tips. The work was hard. Her feet ached, but if she got accepted to the Nursing class, she could work around her classes and in two years, she'd be a nurse. The restaurant was only a few blocks from the college. Determination gave her strength. She would do this or die trying. She hoped that some day Ray would know how she felt. He had no right to do this to the children. They deserved better.

At night, alone in her bed, she often cried. When the children were asleep, she poured her heart out to God. "Lord help me," she prayed, "I still love him. I can't help it, I want him back. My kids need their daddy." She had very little hope left that he would come back. It was more of a way to vent her feelings than it was a prayer that she expected to be answered. At least she no longer lay in bed listening for his car to pull in the drive. That's why she was so shocked when one weekend, he did pull into the driveway. It felt so strange. He just drove up and got out like he owned the place, like he'd just come home from work or something.

"Daddy! Daddy!" The kids were climbing his legs as soon as he was out of the car. Jain's heart skipped a beat, then she took a closer look.

He had lost weight. He looked like he hadn't slept in a while. He was driving an old truck, said he had to trade down after he lost his job. He couldn't find another one. Roni had dumped him and found someone else. He was living with his Mom for the time being, but she was after him to get his own place.

"I want to come home, Jain. I need my kids. Will you take me back?"

She did, but somehow, it wasn't the same. He stayed around the house and worked on his old truck, but he wouldn't keep the kids when she had to work. They made love, but for Jain, something was missing.

It almost felt wrong now. Ray didn't seem to know the difference. She tried harder to make it work. She planned times for the family to be together. Sometimes it almost seemed normal. She convinced herself that she could forgive him and put it all behind her. Her children would have their daddy. They would have a real home again. She still desperately wanted that.

One evening, Jain was raking leaves, the children were playing in he yard, and Ray was washing his truck. It felt almost like they were a real family again, she was almost happy. Things were almost normal. The radio on the truck was playing a popular song. She hummed along, then sang, "Tie a yellow ribbon round the old oak tree—-"

Ray smiled and took a logging chain from behind the seat of his truck. He wrapped it around the oak tree in the edge of the yard and tied it. He had seemed in better spirits the past week. The kids were happier, and Jain had just started to hope that things would be all right again.

"Why did you do that?"

"So that when Roni passes by, she'll see it and she'll know that I still want her. She broke up with her boyfriend." He looked a little sheepish, as he went back to applying polish to his truck.

The song in Jain's heart suddenly died. That particular song would never bring her joy again. He'd made a fool of her once more. She felt so small and useless, not to mention mad. Still, she tried to keep the family together and told herself that it was for the children. She no longer believed in fairy tales.

Ray found a job driving a dump truck. He started comming home late again. Roni and a carload of friends often drove up and down the street, yelling obscenities at Jain.

The neighbors reported it, but nothing was done. Jain had to keep the children inside the house, or in the back yard. Soon the letters started to arrive again.

Ray brought in the mail and tossed it onto the table. There was a letter from Roni, and one from the college. “Why are you getting mail from a college?”

“Oh! Let me see it!” She grabbed it, ignoring the one from Roni. “I can’t believe it! I’ve been accepted. I’m going to be a nurse.” She danced around the living room.

“You’re crazy. You can’t be a nurse. I’m not sending you to school.”

“While you were gone, I got my G.E.D. and applied to nursing school. I’ve been waiting for this for weeks. I’ve been accepted. I can’t believe it. It means that I can make a better life for my kids." She wasn't even aware that she'd started to think of them as hers instead of theirs. This time she didn't hang her head and give up when he put her down. She held on to her dreams. He didn't know how to deal with this.

The next weekend, Ray had a guard drill. He had to leave home by six am and wouldn't be back until six p.m. When Jain got up at five to fix his breakfast, she found another of her 'special delivery' letters. She went to the door when someone knocked, and again, the car sped away as she took the note from her mailbox. I'm sick of this, she thought. My children are asleep in their beds and she is comming onto my porch and putting her notes into my mailbox. She read the note, and the anger inside her was much stronger than the hurt that she still felt. It strengthened her. The note said that Roni and Ray had made love yesterday, and that she couldn't wait to see him again.

He sat down to eat, and she stuck the note in his face. "Is it true?" She went to the sink and took a sip of her coffee.

"Yeah, I guess it is." He sort of laughed.

She threw her coffee cup at him. It shattered on the wall behind his head. Just for a moment, they were both silent. Jain held her breath as she saw the look of furry on his face. It was time for his ride, and she watched as he fought for control. Then he laughed.

"Now Jain, you know you can't live without me."

"You just sit back and watch me! I'll have your things packed when you get home tonight."

He was still laughing when he climbed into the car with his buddies and they headed for the armory. He really believed that she would take anything that he wanted to do to her. He had no feelings, no conscience.

Jain fed the kids, then took them to her sister. "I can't take it any more." She explained all that was going on.

Her sister listened a minute, then said, "I don't know why you took it this long." At that moment, Jain didn't know either. She thought about it all the way home.

Fueled by her anger, she packed everything that he owned into his truck. She put the sideboards on and still it was overflowing. She packed his cloths, his tools, his photographs, and even the furniture that had been given to them by his family. There was barely enough room for him to squeeze beneath the stirring wheel. When he got home that evening, she was waiting by the truck, holding the door open.

The guys were all laughing. Ray was saying something as he was getting out of the car. Suddenly, he froze mid-sentence, his mouth open. The look on his face was priceless. He still had hold of the open car door. Everyone was suddenly silent.

"There's your truck. There's all of your stuff. There's the road, now you hit it!" With hands on her hips, Jain stood her ground and they all knew she meant it.

"Jain, you can't do this!" He was still in shock.

"Ray, I just did it!" She didn't flinch.

He looked from her to his buddies, but Jain stood firm.

With the men in the car still starring with open mouths, he got in his truck and drove away. She took the wedding ring from her finger and threw it after the truck. She watched it bounce down the street, then went inside and cried for hours.

This time, it was easier. It still hurt, but she was stronger. She and the children still had a feast on the day that they got the food stamps, but the rest of the time, she made every penny count. She thanked God that Ray hadn't been back long enough to cause her to loose the help that she was getting. She couldn't believe what a fool she'd been. She vowed that it would never happen again.

She had her own car now, in her name, not his. She wasn't as unprepared as she had been the first time. She felt stronger, but then, a few weeks later she was served with divorce papers. Ray wanted to get the children every weekend, but he didn't want to pay any child support. He also wanted her car and the rest of the furniture. One of his friends from the National

Guard was his lawyer. Jain was frightened. She didn't have a lawyer for a friend. She was afraid that he could take her children. He still had friends on the police force. She had to do something. By now her car was paid for. The bank held the title and loaned her the money to hire a lawyer.

With shaking hands and tears in her eyes, she took the papers to her lawyer. He laughed out loud when he read them. "This is hilarious. He can't do this. Relax Jain it doesn't work that way." Papers were then served on Ray, and a court date was set. Jain's lawyer asked for supervised visitation every other weekend and child support. Ray was furious.

"You won't get a dime from me!" He shouted this for the whole neighborhood to hear. "I'll say they're not mine. I'll get my friends to say they've been with you. Besides, you can't get anything if I don't have a job."

Jain knew that she'd never see any of his money, but she didn't care as long as she had her children. She was afraid of loosing custody. She feared for their safety. She thought that she'd go crazy before this was over. She was living in a nightmare.

When they went to court, Ray's friends did not show. Neither did his family, still, it was awful. Jain's neighbor testified that she was a good mother, that she took good care of the children, that she was crazy for putting up with Ray, but other wise she was a nice person. The people in the courtroom laughed and even the judge smiled a little when she said that. Jain wanted to sink under the seat.

The whole sordid story was made public, even the fact that Roni was only sixteen. Jain was awarded custody of the children, and Ray got supervised visits every other weekend.

Chapter 2

Jain started classes at a small college forty miles from her home. She was now a full time student, but she still had to work. Ray still didn't pay a penny in child support. The waitress job at Shoney's was the only one she could find that let her work around her classes. After a six-hour day at school, she'd go straight to the restaurant, change into her uniform, and work until at least ten. Jain hated the job.

It was hard: Harder than anything she'd ever done before. The worst thing was being away from the children so much. If not for the help of her sister, she would have given up. Everyone told her that she couldn't make it. Sometimes she felt that way herself. She was exhausted. She didn't know how she could go on, and then Brenda said that they could help each other. Her sister was also having problems.

Soon Jain and the kids were living in one room of Brenda's house and sharing the kitchen and the bathroom. Brenda's husband was a truck driver, and was gone most of the time. When he finally did get in, most of his paycheck was gone. Brenda was pregnant and didn't have a job. She watched Cass and Stan while Jain was at work and school. They pooled their resources just to get by. They often counted out the quarters that Jain got as tips to pay the light bill. At least they had enough food, but there was no money for extras. It was hard for all of them.

Cass became sullen and withdrawn, while Stan became loud and demanding. Both children cried for the toys that saw advertised on TV. Stanley desperately wanted a nerf airplane. It only cost a few dollars, but it was money that they didn't have. Jain felt so guilty. She felt guilty for being away from them so much, for not being able to get them the things that they wanted and needed, and especially guilty when they wanted their daddy. She prayed day and night for the Lord to help her get through this and make a better life for her children.

She no longer prayed for Ray to come back. In fact, she thanked God that he was gone. She was determined to make it on her own. She prayed for strength and wisdom.

Sometimes, she wondered if God was listening. She couldn't blame Him if He wasn't. She was no longer able to go to church because she worked every Sunday. She was so very bitter. Sometimes she thought that she hated Ray. This added to her sense of guilt, for she had been a devout Pentecostal prior to her divorce.

Now, she lived in a strange and different world. Sometimes she felt so lost. Still, she cared about people. She was a giving person. She wanted to help. That was one of the reasons why she wanted to be a nurse, that and the job security. There was always a shortage of nurses.

Her nursing class started out with one hundred and four students. Some were Jain's age. A few were older, but most were in their twenties. Each had a different background, a different life style. Jain made new friends. She had to. She almost never saw her old ones anymore. When she did, she felt odd, like she was an outsider, a third wheel. They were still married and they always had news of Ray and Roni and they always seemed delighted to share it.

By the end of the first quarter, she had two close friends and the class was down to sixty-five. Some had dropped out, some had failed, and Jain only had a C average in Nursing. She was making A's and B's in everything else. Still, she was determined to make it. She had to; She had the children to think about. They deserved better.

She felt so inadequate and insecure. She cried to her family, but they couldn't understand. She prayed harder. At night she cried into her pillow. She talked to anyone who would listen, but few wanted to hear her troubles. No one understood what she was going through. Their attitude was, get over it, but for Jain, it was easier said than done.

"Why don't you quit school and live on Medicaid, stay home with your kids?"

Or "Why don't you just find someone else to marry that will help you with the bills and the kids?" they wanted to know. Jain felt like a beggar and a low life as it was, and though she tried not to let it show, she was still hurt. Sometimes she felt like she was the nothing and nobody that Ray had always said she was.

Someone told her that Ray and Roni had finally gotten married, and that he seemed very happy. They said that he looked ten years younger and was always smiling. Her Mom ran into them at the grocery store. She told Jain that Roni was very friendly, and that she seemed like a really sweet person. It hurt, but not as much as she had thought it would. Besides, Ray didn't act all that married, nor for that matter, all that happy, when Jain saw him.

He'd started coming to Shoney's when she was working, usually with two or three other men. Jain didn't have to wait on him, others would do it for her, but she could feel his eyes burning into her back. She could feel his hatred for her, and it made her nervous. Once, she broke a glass because she was so upset.

One Saturday evening, he came in with just one other man. They both sat at the bar, drinking coffee and starred at Jain. She felt very uneasy. It wasn't the way Ray starred at her, she was getting used to that, but his friend also starred at her with hatred in his eyes. He had the coldest, steele blue eyes that she'd ever seen. She cringed when their gaze met. He never blinked, nor looked away. They left after about thirty minutes and relief washed over her like a welcome flood. She felt safer with them gone.

It was her night to close, which meant she would be the last one to leave. Thank God, she had the next day off. They locked the doors at two am, but she had to wash down the tables and booths. She finished, locked up, and went out to the parking lot, which was now empty, except for her old car. She started it up and headed for home, thinking of sleeping late, then spending time with the kids. She would take them to play in the creek, pack a picnic lunch and make a day of it.

The streets were almost deserted. Another car, which was parked across the street, fell in behind her and followed her out of town. It stayed close on her bumper. At first, she thought nothing of it, but the lights were on bright and reflected in her rearview mirror. This began to bother her, so out on the highway, she speeded up. So did the other car. On a long, straight stretch, she slowed to let it pass. It didn't, but stayed on her bumper. She speeded up again. The other car stayed with her. She was beginning to get frightened. All the houses were dark. All the stores were closed, and by now, she was about half way between home and work. She kept driving.

"He will stop when we get into town." She told herself. He didn't. She drove by City hall, but there was no one in site. She remembered the nights that she had looked everywhere for Ray and found no one. There would be no help from the police in this town. She turned onto the highway to go home. He followed. She turned onto the dirt road where she lived. So did he. Jain was near panic.

"What will I do?" she wondered. "I can't lead him to my children and my sister."

Her headlights shinned on the house, and then she knew! There, tied to the cloths line in front of the house was Cain. The German Shepherd that belonged to her brother-in-law could be vicious, but he loved Jain. She rolled the window down and spoke to the dog, then she slid out of the car and grabbed his collar. She had him loose by the time the other car pulled in front of hers and stopped. The man with the cold, steele eyes got out and stood starring at her. She saw the knife that he held behind one leg only because the moonlight happened to reflect on it.

"That dog won't bite, will he?" His voice was smooth, emotionless.

"He will tear you to pieces." Jain's voice was shaky. As if to back her up, Cain turned every hair on his body the wrong way and gave the most vicious growl that Jain had ever heard. His teeth were barred.

The man put one foot forward and the dog lunged. He uttered a curse word, jumped into his car and slammed the door. Cain was looking through the window, paws on the door and teeth gleaming as the car roared to life. Gravel flew as the car sped away. The dog was unharmed.

Shaking, Jain sank to the ground. Cain came for his hug, tail wagging, but Jain needed the comfort more than the dog did. When she could move, she went to the house. She opened the door to find Brenda, standing in the dark, holding the shotgun. They let Cain run loose that night. Both were frightened, but tried not to show it.

"Who on earth was that?"

"I don't know. He was with Ray at the restaurant. He was waiting for me when I started home." She told the rest of the story. Sleep was impossible now, so they talked.

"They're just trying to scare you."

Brenda was trying to make her feel better, but she wasn't very convincing. They watched for hours, but the man didn't come back. Still, the uneasy feeling stayed with them. The next day, Jain didn't let the children out of her site. Brenda spent the day with their Mom. The man didn't come back, but Ray called and asked if she had a good night.

On Monday, Jain found a new job working in a shirt factory. She worked the evening shift, three to eleven. Now she at least had the weekend with the children.

She had a little more money now, and as Brenda's due date drew closer, her husband was home more. There's a lot of truth to the old saying, "one house wasn't built for two families," and no matter how close the sisters were, they were feeling the strain. Jain and the kids would ride around and look for a place to live on Saturdays. They were on a waiting list to get into a housing project. Finally, they got a two bedroom duplex. The kids were so excited. Jain slept on the sofa and let them each have a room to themselves.

They unpacked the things that had been stored in boxes for months. It felt so good to have their own home again!

They had a new routine. Jain worked the three to eleven shift at the shirt factory.

She still went straight to work from school, but she now had the weekend with the kids.

They also had a little more money. Jain got her mother to baby-sit for twenty-five dollars a week. She made a new friend, Lucy, who really did listen to her problems. Lucy didn't think that Jain was crazy for trying to be a nurse. She encouraged her, and even signed up for some classes herself. Jain's life was hectic, but she found more and more happy moments. She smiled now, as often as she frowned. She enjoyed her time with her friends as well as her time with her children. The pace never slowed, but she was getting used to it. She was beginning to thrive on it.

Payday came and at lunch, Jain picked up her check and rushed to get it cashed.

She had to get gas before she went home. The tank was on empty. She also wanted to buy something for the children. In her rush, she left the gas cap laying on the pump at the service station. She bought a nerf airplane for Stan and a new Barbie for Cass and barely made it back to class without being late. She didn't realize that she'd lost her gas cap until two days later, when she had to get gas again. By then, she didn't have enough money to get another one.

"Oh well," she said to herself, "I can do without a gas cap until payday." She wasn't too upset. It seemed like a minor problem.

Friday came and she was tired and in a hurry to get home. She forgot about the gas cap again. She picked up the kids and was home by midnight. They walked into the house, still half asleep. Jain tucked them into their beds, locked up, and was asleep as soon as her head hit her pillow.

Suddenly she was awakened by a loud noise. She heard men cursing loudly, just outside her window. Her first thoughts were that Ray was up to something. She sat up and looked out the window. What she saw was almost as frightening. Her neighbor and several other men were staggering around and around her car, lighting cigarettes and flicking lighted matches and cigarette buts everywhere. She knew they were drunk.

"Oh God! I didn't get the gas cap!"

She jumped to her feet at once. She stuck her head out the door and yelled, "Get away from that car! It doesn't have a gas cap!"

Startled, they stopped and starred. One called her a bad name, but they broke up the group. Her neighbor staggered into his house and the others left. Jain fell asleep to the sound of her neighbors fighting. Still, it was good to be home. She and the kids slept until ten a.m., then ate breakfast in front of the TV.

Just when Jain had decided that it was a wonderful day, she heard someone knocking on the door. The kids rushed to open it, and there stood Ray.

Jain sighed, then told him to come on in and visit with the kids. She picked up the dirty dishes and carried them into the kitchen. As she washed the dishes, she listened to her children trying to talk to their dad. Stan tried to show him his new airplane. Ray only grunted and nodded a few times. Stan soon gave up and went into his room to play with his toys, but Cass kept on trying. Ray left her talking, and came to the kitchen door. With her head dropped and her bottom lip stuck out, Cass finally gave up and went to her room. Ray started to rant and rave at Jain.

"You think you are so smart, but you'll see." His voice grew louder as he talked.

"My life is a mess because of you. I'll make you pay! You will never be a nurse."

"Look Ray, you are free. You have Roni. Everyone says you are happy now. If you want to see the kids, visit with them. If not, you just need to go."

She saw his knuckles grow white where he gripped the door facing. He uttered a string of curse words as he took a step toward her. Just then, someone knocked loudly on the wall that separated the houses.

"Keep it down in there! I've got a headache!" a man's voice boomed.

Ray gave her a hateful look, but backed off. Jain smiled. Duplexes weren't so bad after all. Thank God that Ray cared about what other people thought of him.

Ray left without even saying goodbye to the kids, but he had somehow managed to take the joy out of the day. It took hours to get the children in a good mood again.

She took them to the creek. Soon their laughter rang out as they splashed in the water and fed stale bread to the minnows. Life began to stir and bubble inside Jain again. She no longer felt dead, tired yes, but not dead. Time had passed and healing had started. It felt good to be alive.

Chapter 3

Life in the housing project was different, but not too bad. It was, after all, a very small town, small enough that a divorce still caused a scandal. There were a few fights. The police were called out once in awhile for a domestic disturbance, and there were thefts, but nothing that was shocking to Jain. No murders were ever committed. Other than the drunks, drugs were not a problem. It was the way of life that she knew.

Jain had been surprised to learn that her being divorced hardly mattered to her new acquaintances in a town just forty miles away. Even here at home, things were beginning to change. People, who had looked down their noses at her a year ago, now looked at her like she was a puzzle to them. She'd catch bits of their conversations as she and the kids walked by. "You mean she's really going back to school? At her age?" Or: "I didn't really think she could do it." This no longer upset her. She now felt more sorry for some of them than they did for her. To a certain extent, she even understood why they felt that way. She was growing and gaining new insights as she slowly came back to life. She had seen other women get divorced and go from man to man, looking for a home that they never seemed to find. Jain knew now why they did that, but before, she didn't have so much empathy for them. Loneliness was a mean companion, and change was hard, but she felt herself growing stronger.

The kids were also gaining new values. They were making new friends, and as fate would have it, a few new enemies. The houses in the project made a large semi circle. Stan didn't always get along well with the little boy that lived directly across from them. The boy, Billy, had a habit of taking any of Stan's toys that he could find. Stan made it a point to get them back. Sometimes they played together and sometimes they fought. Stan had a blue quilt with multicolored butterflies on it that no one else was allowed to touch. One Friday morning, Jain did the laundry and hung it on the cloths line before she left for school and work. She thought it would give her more time with the children over the weekend. Stan's quilt would take a long time to dry.

The next morning, Stan was shaking her awake. "Unlock the door and let me out! Billy has my quilt and I'm going to get it."

Jain looked out the window. There, across the pavement, staked out into a tent, was the butterfly quilt. She grabbed her robe, unlocked the door, and followed Stan across the pavement. He pulled the nails that held his quilt in the ground, wadded up his quilt, stuck it under his arms, and for good measure, kicked over the wooden stakes that held up the center. She repaired and rewashed the quilt, and they stayed home all day waiting for it to dry.

Ray's visits were few and far between now. The kids no longer stayed by the window waiting for him to come by on every weekend. Jain thanked God for that. They played with the neighborhood kids. Some of them had bikes and Stan and Cass wanted bikes desperately. Jain couldn't afford them. Work had slowed at the factory and she was back to barely getting by. This served as a reminder of why she was trying to become a nurse. There was no one to turn to for help.

"Why don't you take Ray back to court and make him pay the child support?" Brenda asked.

Jain tried to explain that she didn't want to get things stirred up again. Besides, she didn't have the time, energy, or money to do it. She couldn't miss time from classes.

Ray wouldn't pay it anyway. She reminded Brenda that he hadn't supported them when they were married. Now that he and Roni were expecting a baby, he probably did have a job, but Jain remembered his threats. By now, she believed that she could make it. Even though she almost never got to church, she prayed desperately. Sometimes at night, she still cried into her pillow to keep the kids from hearing her. Time no longer seemed to stand still, but moved along at a faster pace. Jain was almost frantic, trying to keep up.

Determination as well as exhaustion and desperation sometimes showed on her face. She still had only a C average in Nursing. She would often just sit on the bench outside the classroom door and rest after her morning classes. She had just started fifth quarter.

They called it the make or break quarter. Everyone said that if you made it through fifth quarter, you had it made. Many students failed it each year. One morning, she collapsed on the bench after class. Exhaustion weighed heavy on her shoulders, and she was worried about loosing her job. The factory had started sending them home early almost every night. She'd been through this before, and she feared a layoff. She wouldn't be able to draw unemployment and go to school full time.

When the last student left, the instructor stuck her head out and said, “Jain, I need to see you please.”

Her first thought was that she was failing. They’d had a test the day before and the grades weren’t yet posted. She entered the room with a heavy heart.

“Jain, I’m concerned about you. You always look so tired. You don’t socialize enough with your peers. I wondered if it might help to talk I know that you have a C average, but you have more empathy for the patients than anyone in the class. I would like to know what’s going on.”

Jain told her. She didn’t know what else to do, and she just couldn’t give up now.

She found a new support person. The instructor had a friend who was D.O.N. at a nursing home. Jain soon had a job working weekends again, but this time, it was days. She worked three evenings a week also.

Now there were only three nights a week that she felt deprived of her children. She even had more time to study after the children were in bed.

It was time that she desperately needed. She was barely passing.

Nursing class was harder than ever. It was no longer studying one body system at a time, nor one disease and the treatment for it. It was now how all body systems were affected when one was sick. It was how the respiratory system affected the cardiac system. It was fluids and electrolytes. It was body chemistry and diet. It was drugs and their side effects. It was all the things that could go wrong with a person all rolled into one. It was how treating one problem could complicate another one, even put a person into a crisis. It was frightening. So many things could go wrong. She started to learn about the psychological aspects of nursing. Still, she struggled along. She even managed to put a couple of bicycles on lay away for Christmas. Stan and Cass were going to be surprised.

Jain wasn't the only person who was sweating over grades. At least a third of the class would pass or fail depending on their grade on the final test. It counted sixty percent of the total grade. Everyone was nervous. Some students were in tears at the end of the day. They all crammed for the test. The dreaded day finally came. It was a Thursday. They took the test and went home. The grades wouldn't be posted until the next day.

There was a crowd outside the nursing building the next morning when Jain arrived. She sat on the bench. She didn't have the courage to go look at the grades. She watched her peers as they came and went. She heard their cries of "YES!" when they found that they had made it. She saw some leave in tears. The instructor who had taken an interest in her came by.

"Jain, have you looked at the grades yet?"

"No." Jain shook her head and the instructor walked away. Five minutes later, she was back.

"Jain, go look at the grades. You will like it." She went back in the room.

Jain felt hope stir inside her. She stood on wobbly knees, and slowly made her way to the board where the grades were posted. By now, the crowd had dwindled to only a few. She took a deep breath and looked at the list. She had passed the quarter by two points! They had only lost five students.

"Oh thank you, God!" her heart cried, for she knew that without His help, she would not have made it this far. She felt like celebrating.

She found Lucy, who treated her to lunch, then she went and got the bicycles off lay away and took them home. How on earth was she going to hide them until Christmas?

Finally, she decided to put them into the kitchen closet. She moved everything out, put the bicycles in, and nailed the door shut. She was waiting when the kids got off the bus at her Mom's, and took them out for hamburgers. She still felt like celebrating. The kids were in a good mood and hungry.

She had a week out of school before she started her sixth quarter. She still had to work, but still, she had a few days at home. She got to know the woman next door. At first, the woman would barely answer when Jain spoke to her. They gradually increased their conversations while they hung cloths on the line. One morning, her neighbor came out with a black eye. Jain had heard the fight the night before. She'd seen the police come and leave, taking no one with them. She'd seen the man leave for work that morning, as if nothing had happened. Until recently, she had thought this was a normal way of life.

"Why do you stay with him?" Jain asked the question, though she knew the answer. She had done the same.

She heard all the usual answers. I have no place to go. I have no way to support my children. He would kill me if I left him. The police won't help, they say it's a domestic problem. It just makes it worse when someone calls them. I love him.

Jain told her about her own life, how she'd been through some of the same things. The most frightening thing was that Jain knew if Ray hadn't left her, she'd still be in that same situation. It was a sobering thought. She wanted to help her neighbor, but she didn't know how. It was all she could do to survive and take care of the kids. With her determination stronger than ever, she continued her education. Things seemed to be a little easier. She made B's now. She had less than a year to go and a lighter class load.

Thanksgiving week came and she had a little extra time with the kids. One morning, she left them inside and went out to get the mail. As she opened the door to go back inside, she saw Stan, hammer still in hand, eyes wide and mouth open. The nails from the kitchen closet lay at his feet.

"Cass! Look! Bicycles!"

Jain was speechless. She could tell that Cass didn't believe her brother, but she got up and looked inside the closet. Then Jain saw her eyes light up. They were laughing as they dragged the bikes out the door. Jain had a fleeting thought that she didn't know what she'd do for Christmas, but today was wonderful. The children were so happy. Jain cherished each moment of their happiness. They were still so sad most of the time.

Brenda stopped by with a copy of the local paper. On the society page, she saw a picture of Ray and Roni's new baby, a little girl. The children saw it also. Later that day, someone asked Cass how she liked her new baby sister. Both children were upset. They asked hard questions, like, "Why does Ray like that baby and not us." Jain didn't have an answer. She told them that there was something missing in Ray, something that kept him from feeling love like most people do. She told them that it wasn't their fault, that any normal person would be happy to have them. She told them how much she loved them. It didn't really help. She felt the hatred for Ray building up inside her. God help me, she silently cried, I can forgive him for what he did to me, but he's hurt my children. She felt so far away from God at times like this. She also realized that the children now called Ray by his given name more often than they called him daddy. She couldn't blame them. He certainly didn't act like any daddy she'd ever known. Now it seemed that he only showed up when he and Roni were having problems. Jain had made up her mind that she wasn't going to take any more of his verbal abuse, and she sure wasn't going to let him hit her ever again. If only she could stop him from hurting her children. At least he didn't come around as much these days.

On Friday evening, they went to the grocery. Just outside the entrance, a crowd was gathered. Too late, Jain saw that it was Ray, Roni, and the new baby.

People were stopping to admire the baby. As Jain and the children walked up to the entrance, Ray glared at her. He glanced at the children, but didn't speak. He put his arm around Roni and tickled the baby under the chin. Jain ushered the children into the store. Ray and Roni were gone when they came out. The kids were far too quiet for the rest of the day. Jain had a feeling that there was worse to come. The next morning, Ray was pounding on her door.

"You just have to cause trouble for me, don't you. You can't stand for anyone to be happy. I ought to beat you into a pulp! You've made Roni upset. If I had five hundred dollars, you'd be dead!" His fists were clenched. He was filled with rage.

Jain had only opened the door a crack. She started to close it. He stuck his foot in so that she couldn't.

She felt fear, but she wasn't going to let him know that.

"What are you talking about? I don't bother you. It's not my problem if you are not happy. If you want to see the kids, come back when you calm down." She tried again to close the door.

He shoved it open and walked in over her. The kids baseball bat was lying on the floor and she grabbed it. The look on her face told him she'd use it. They were at a standoff. Jain tried not to let her fear show. The neighbors had moved away, but maybe Ray didn't know that. He still put up a good front in public.

"You are never going to hit me again. I don't have to take this from you. We are divorced. This is my home, you need to go to yours."

Just then, the mailman walked onto the porch and knocked. He had a package that wouldn't fit into the box.

"Ms. Davis, you have a package. Is everything ok?"

Ray laughed a little and reached for the package. When the postman held onto it, and looked at Jain, Ray turned on his heel and left.

Jain breathed a sigh of relief, then checked on the children. They were still asleep. Ray didn't come back. Later that evening, Jain heard that Roni had fallen down the stairs and was bruised up pretty bad. Ray had taken her to the doctor, but she wasn't seriously hurt. Everyone talked about how concerned Ray was and how he stayed right by her side and told her in front of everyone how much he loved her. It gave Jain an eerie feeling.

Jain had so few weekends off and this one was pretty much ruined. Anger threatened to consume her. She kept the kids inside, playing games and watching television. They would just stay home and try to relax. Sunday morning, while the kids slept in, she listened to the TV preachers. They talked about forgiveness, forgiving your enemies. She tried. God, how she tried, but she knew she hadn't been able to do it. She felt like she couldn't go to church with all the bitterness that was in her heart. She missed it though, all the good singing, the revivals, the dinners, the preaching, but most of all she missed the closeness that she used to feel to God. It felt like a part of her was missing, like she was thirsty and couldn't get filled. She couldn't really put her feelings into words. Even on good days, when things were going right, it felt like wanting a good, cold milkshake and having to settle for a glass of tepid water. She ran into a friend of hers that she hadn't seen in years. He was a preacher.

"Where do you go to church now?"

"I don't"

"What? I can't believe that. What happened?"

"I got divorced. I have so many bad feelings. I'm not really living it. I'd feel like a hypocrite if I went to church. People look down on me and I just feel like I shouldn't go. I'm not sure I belong in a church right now."

He took a step backward and looked at her with mock surprise.

"Lord no, Jain!" He shook his head. "If you're dirty, don't go anywhere near a bathtub!"

Jain felt better after talking to him, but she still couldn't bring herself to go to church. She was slowly drifting further and further away from God. Years later, she would look back and realize that God had never forsaken her, even in her present state of mind, she knew that she couldn't make it without him. She still prayed each night and asked for His help and thanked Him for her children.

The children recovered faster now from the setbacks caused by the divorce. They seemed stronger and older than most kids their age. They were doing well in school. Cass had a best friend who often spent the night when Jain could be home. Cass spent nights when Jain worked with her friend about once every two weeks.

Even though she felt incomplete, life went on. She loved her job. The children were healthy, and for the most part, happy. Men sometimes asked her to go out, but she couldn't fit dating into her life. It was tempting, though. When I get through school, she thought, then I'll get a life. She sometimes felt like her life was suspended in limbo. She had been traveling through this dark valley for so long. At times like this, she had to look back and see how far she had already come. Winter was a hard time, but it would pass.

She had learned how to drive in the snow. She'd never done it until she'd had to.

There were only two snows big enough to cause hazardous driving conditions last winter.

She had made it to her destination safely both times, still, it made her nervous when she had to drive on the icy roads. She would have to do it anyway, there was no other choice.

They were always short handed at the nursing home, and the college didn't close due to weather. One evening she went to work, and while she was there, it snowed four inches.

Most of the midnight girls called in, and Jain had to work a double shift. As soon as the day shift arrived, she prepared to head home.

She was exhausted and she'd never been so sleepy in all her life. She had two cups of coffee before she left, and then washed her face in cold water. As she left the building, she caught her breath. The entire world seemed to be covered with a thick, white blanket. She had to guess where the road went. She was so afraid that she would slide off the road and flip her car. There were no tracks to drive in; she was breaking the trail toward home. The salt trucks had not yet run. She drove slowly, every muscle tensed, all her nerves taunt. She really resented Ray at times like this.

She made it half way home before she plowed into a bank. She was lucky, because on the other side of the road, there was a ten-foot drop off. When the car hit the bank, her head hit the windshield. The next thing she knew, an ambulance had arrived and the EMT was knocking on the window. She had no idea who had called them. Her head hurt and things seemed fuzzy. For just a moment, she didn't know what had happened.

"Mam, are you alright?" The man had opened the door and was shinning a light in her eyes.

She surveyed the damage. "My car! How will I get home to my children? I don't know what I'll do now."

"Mam, we have to take you to the hospital or to the doctors office of your choice to be checked out."

Jain forced herself to think. "Take me to my doctor." She gave them the address. The ambulance personnel were also kind enough to call the wrecker service from her hometown to come and get her car.

Thank God no other vehicles were involved. She had no insurance.

After she was examined and told to go home and rest, she called her sister to come and get her. They went to check out the damage to the car.

"I'm afraid it's totaled." the mechanic told her. "We can give you thirty five dollars plus the wrecker bill and sell it for junk."

"No!" Jain almost yelled at him. "I paid more than that for the tires."

"Sorry Mam, it's the best we can do."

"Will it still run?" Jain was desperate.

"Well, yes. It runs, but the frame is bent. You'd have to have a new fender, fix the radiator. It will never run right. It's best to junk it and get another one."

"I can't! It's not possible. I don't have insurance. I have to have my car."

In the end, she talked him into fixing the radiator. He bent the fender out enough that it didn't rub into the tire, and Jain drove the car home. It took every cent that she had to pay the wrecker bill and the repair bill. The kids were upset when they saw it.

"What happened to the car?" Cass wanted to know.

"You made the car curly!" Stan accused. He really loved the car. He was mad for two days. They drove the car with the bent frame and crumpled fender for six more months, until Jain got out of school and could trade it. Still, she wouldn't have made it if she hadn't applied for and gotten a student loan. God must have meant for her to be a nurse.

In the spring, Jain graduated from nursing school, and Stan graduated from kindergarten. Cass finished forth grade. Jain got a job working as a graduate nurse, midnight shift in the small hospital in her hometown. They paid off her loan and she singed a contract to work there for at least two years. She had a hard time sleeping days.

The children had to play quietly inside or watch TV while she slept. They weren't allowed to go outside until she got up. They went through yet another period of adjustment.

Jain passed state boards the first time that she took them and made a much higher score than she had thought she could. The children became familiar with hospital life. If Jain got called in to work on her nights off, or if she didn't have a babysitter, the children slept in an empty hospital room. She felt like she'd lived a dozen lifetimes in one. She knew that the kids must feel the same. To her surprise, they seemed to become more secure and well adjusted. They were much better at adjusting than she could ever be.

Chapter 4

When you work in a small town hospital, sooner or later, you see everything. There were slow nights when there were only a few patients and it was hard to stay awake. There were others when Jain didn't stop all night. There would be one emergency right after another. Besides being the midnight charge nurse, she had to cover the E R. In the thirty two bed hospital, the night shift consisted of one RN, one LPN, and one aide.

Days and evening shifts had more help. The reasoning was that they had to do baths and meals. They also usually had more meds to pass. People were supposed to sleep on midnights. In reality, it didn't work that way. When people were sick, they were sicker at night. Temperatures went higher at night.

People were more congested at night. Pains were exacerbated at night They had sick babies in croup tents. They had patients from the nursing home to get sick and come to the hospital per ambulance at midnight. They had to do labor and delivery because babies were often born on midnight shift. Emergency surgeries had to be done on midnights. When someone came to the ER at midnight, it was often a true emergency. Lab and Xray technicians had to be called in on midnights. OB and the surgery nurses could also be called in, but often the babies didn't wait for the OB nurse to get there. Doctors were tired and wanted to sleep at night, but they also had to be called in at night. Sometimes Jain had to call the doctor all night long, knowing that he would have to be in his clinic all the next day.

The police sometimes brought in intoxicated people that they had found driving, to have blood alcohols drawn. That was easy. Their veins were full and easy to stick. They were usually feeling no pain and even in a good mood. If they were combative instead, the police cuffed them.

Sometimes, the police would swing by for a free cup of coffee. The café's all closed at ten. Jain got to know some of them and found that they were not all like Ray. Some of them knew Ray, but didn't like him. Some were still his buddies. They said things like; "You must have changed. You're nothing at all like Ray said you were."

Jain ignored those remarks. The nurses and police depended on each other. A free cup of coffee seemed like a small price to pay for the help they sometimes gave. If they saw a stranger milling around, or heard unexplained noises outside, they could call city hall and a car would be there in five minutes. If they needed to get hold of a nurse that didn't have a phone, or one who had the phone off the hook, the police would go and tell the nurse that she was needed at the hospital.

Jain found this out on one of her first Saturday nights off. She had stayed up all day with the children. By eight o'clock she was exhausted, and she put the kids to bed. She was asleep as soon as her head hit the pillow. At twelve-thirty, she was awakened by a loud pounding on the door. She jumped up, grabbed her robe, and almost passed out when she looked through the window. A policeman, one that she didn't know, stood pounding on her door. She managed to get the door open. Her knees trembled, her hands shook, and her face was pale.

"What's wrong?" She was frightened, but she knew her children were safe and asleep in their beds.

"Nothing's wrong, Miss Davis. I didn't mean to scare you. They need you to come to work. There's been a wreck with multiple injuries. The hospital is full because of the flu epidemic, but they said to tell you that you can bring the children and put them to bed on the sofas in the lounge."

The nurse that lived inside her took over. She was like a different person in her role as nurse. She bundled the kids in warm clothing, got into her uniform, and was at the hospital in thirty minutes. The aide found blankets and settled the kids in the lounge and Jain went straight to work. There were wounds to clean and dress, IV's to start, histories to take, and meds to give. The doctor was on his way, but he had already given phone orders. Xray and lab personnel were already there.

There were six patients in the emergency room. Three were treated and sent home and three were admitted to the hospital. They had to move patients around to make room for the new admissions. Two men that had been in separate rooms had to be moved in together. That made a room for the two men that were in the pickup, one had fractured ribs and the other had a head injury. The one with the fractured ribs would be monitored for any signs and symptoms of respiratory distress and congestion. The one with the head injury would need pupil checks, and to be monitored for any changes in mental status. Jain would do this every fifteen minutes for an hour, then every two hours until she went home and the next shift took over.

They set up a bed in the end of a hall and found a portable curtain to provide privacy for the woman who was a passenger in the car. Her injuries were less painful, but she'd lost a lot of blood. She had IV fluids and antibiotics to replace the fluid loss and to prevent the cuts from becoming infected. As Jain helped her get into a hospital gown, she noticed older, fading bruises on the woman's body. They couldn't have come from the accident. She remembered how insistent the woman's husband had been when he tried to get the doctor to send his wife home.

"How'd you get these bruises on your back?"

"Must have been from the wreck."

The woman didn't want to talk about it. Jain didn't confront her, but she noted it in the chart. When she went to the nurses' station, she mentioned it to the other nurse.

“Oh, she comes in about once a month or so. Everyone knows that her husband beats her, but she won’t do anything about it.”

“She must like it, or she wouldn’t put up with it.” Someone else joined in.

Jain’s temper flared. “She doesn’t like it! She’s caught in a trap, like an animal!”

“Whoa! Jain, what’s gotten into you?”

Jain told them a little of what she’d been through. She also apologized for letting her personal feelings get in the way.

“I don’t believe it,” said the aide. “I know Ray, and he wouldn’t do something like that. I dated him before he married Roni.”

“Well, believe what you want.” Jain told her. “What really scares me, is that I might still be caught in that situation if Ray hadn’t left me.”

She went to check on her patients and finish her charting. She also had to put the charts together. There was no ward clerk on midnights. She had a patient come in with a migraine headache, who was treated and observed for thirty minutes, then released.

By the time the day shift arrived, things were quiet. Jain took the kids home, fixed them breakfast, turned on the television, locked the door, and told them to wake her in two hours or if they really needed her. She had never been so tired.

She was dreaming. In her dream, Ray was shaking her. She could feel his fingers biting into her arm. She could see the snarl on his lips and the hatred in his eyes. In the background, she could hear a woman laughing; saying Ray wouldn't do that. It's your fault Jain, your fault. She groaned. Groggily she opened her eyes to find Stan shaking her awake.

"Moma, I'm hungry. You said you were gonna sleep two hours."

She looked at the clock. She had slept half the day. She forced herself out of bed and washed her face and hands, then she followed Stan into the kitchen. Cass sat at the table drawing.

"I told him to let you sleep."

"No, I needed to get up. If I had slept all day, I wouldn't have slept tonight. I meant to be up hours ago." After lunch, they went to visit family.

She sat on her Mom's porch and watched the children play. She watched as Brenda and her husband came across the field, hand in hand, from the creek where they had been catching minnows to use for fish bait. She knew that their marriage wasn't perfect, but today, they were happy. Jain was miserable. She had never felt so alone and out of place. She thought of her friend, Sam, who'd been asking her out for weeks.

"Mom, do you remember Sam? He had a crush on me when I was fifteen. He's been asking me out. Do you think I should go out with him?"

"I've been telling you for years, Jain. You need to get married and stay home with your children. They need a daddy. Sam's not good looking and he doesn't have much money, but I believe he'd be good to you and the children. Of course you'd have to raise his kids. They are spoiled rotten."

It was true that Sam lived for his children, but Jain did the same.

"Mom, I'm not talking about marriage, I just get so lonesome sometimes."

People at work encouraged Jain to date again. Because she was so lonely, she finally agreed to go out with Sam. It was a disaster, worse than staying home alone. They took the children, both his and hers, and went out to eat. His kids pulled at him and hers pulled at her. It was like they were in a war. A line was clearly drawn, with Jain and her children on one side and Sam and his on the other. Cass and Stan resented him and made no effort to hide it. His three boys felt the same about Jain. As if that weren't enough, the kids didn't like each other. They argued about where they sat in the car, about where they were going to eat, and even who looked the 'dorkiest'. It felt like there was a great gap between them filled with hostility, unseen but very much felt. It was very awkward; still they tried it a few more times before they gave up.

Eventually, Sam found someone else and Jain slipped back into her rut. She was disappointed, not because of loosing Sam, but because she wanted something more from life. She was so tired of being alone.

She dumped her feelings on Lucy. Lucy and her husband had started going to a square dance every Saturday night. She told Jain that she ought to start going there.

“It’s a lot of fun, and you can bring the kids. I know how you are about those kids. They don’t serve alcohol. Families go there, but there are singles too. You might meet someone. You need to get out more.”

It worked! The kids loved it. They found friends their own age, and Jain learned to dance. Lucy was right. There were a few single men there, and when Jain wasn’t on the dance floor, she enjoyed sitting with Lucy and listening to the music and watching the others dance. Her children were naturals. They had rhythm. Jain did not. Sometimes they had a Buck

Dance contest for kids. Stan won it. The prize was five dollars. From then on, every time that she had a Saturday off, that's where they went. Jain's Mom and sisters started going there also, and it was even more fun. It was years before the kids tired of the dance. They seldom made other plans for their Saturdays.

Without realizing it, Jain was slipping further and further away from God and the life that she had once lived. It was a gradual thing. She still prayed. She loved her children and she loved her work, but she still didn't go to church. The emptiness inside her grew larger. She tried in vain to fill it. She filled her life with her children, her work, and now with the dance on Saturday nights.

At first, even if she had danced with the same man all night, and had known him for awhile, she left him at midnight. She and the kids went home alone and she would not tell any of her dance partners where she lived. She thought that she was finally over Ray. She often felt the desire that had been rekindled inside her as she slow danced with a handsome man. Sometimes it was hard not to give in to temptation. Loneliness and unfulfillmemt often kept her awake all night. Still, life was sometimes fun again. She was almost happy. The children were older and happier. They almost never mentioned Ray. They didn't seem to care as much that he wasn't around.

Time had raced by again. Jain wondered where it had gone and how it had passed so quickly. She was now working evening shift at the hospital. It was great, except that she was often going to work just when the kids were coming home from school. She missed them. They got off the bus at their grandmother's, and Jain picked them up at eleven thirty.

Now that the children were older, they wanted more freedom and distance from their Mom. Cass had a boyfriend! She wasn't old enough to date, but she danced with him almost every Saturday night. If Jain had to work, Cass and Stan went to the dance with family, or with Lucy. Jain felt a new emptiness in her heart. She filled it with work.

Patients who were in the hospital a lot, called Jain by her given name. Some of them had known her all her life. Most knew her parents. Jain loved interacting with them. She wanted to make a difference in their lives. The people that she worked with were now like family. Because of the nature of the job, she often felt closer to them than she did to her relatives. They counted on each other, the nurses, the doctors, the aides, and even the people who worked in the kitchen and the offices. They were a team, a family, but they were even more than that. They held people's lives in their hands and they earned their trust. The kept confidentiality's and tried to be objective. They stood at death's door and fought to keep people alive.

The enemy was infections, heart attacks, life threatening injuries, accidents, suicides, and the worst of all for Jain was cancer. Cancer was a battle that was often lost. When that was the case, they tried to ease the pain and keep the patient comfortable. Sometimes surgery could save a life, but some cancers were inoperable. No matter what the prognosis, the word cancer filled a patient with fear. You could see the panic in their eyes at the mention of the word. It spilled over into their families and friends. They all looked at you with eyes filled with desperation, silently pleading for you to do something.

Grace was a patient who had colon cancer. She was well known to the staff, because she also had a heart condition and had been in and out of the hospital often. Jain had gotten close to her and knew her life's story. She knew that Grace had married her husband when she was only sixteen years old. They had eloped. Burt had slipped to her window after dark, and they had run away and gotten married. He had carried her across the creek, because Grace had on a new dress and pair of shoes that she didn't want to get wet. They'd been together ever since. They had reared six children, who had all "turned out well" except for one son who was in prison. Now Grace and Burt had his twelve-year-old son living with them. They were colorful and happy and Grace had wormed her way deep into Jain's heart.

One evening, Jain got out of report and started toward the nurse's station. Grace met her half way down the hall, pushing her I.V on a pole. Usually, Grace was happy, but not today.

“Did you know I’ve got cancer?”

Jain nodded and put her arm around Grace’s shoulder and walked her back to her room. She settled Grace on the bed and sat in the chair to listen. Grace was mad at the other nurses. The only two that she really liked were Jain and Dana, the daytime charge nurse. These two, she called by first name.

“They kept Dana in the ER all day. The rest of them don’t care. They just tell me I’ll be all right. If I’m not, what will happen to Freddie? He may be my grandson, but I’m all he’s got. I need to live to get him grown.”

Jain could identify with that. She often had the same fears about her own children. She let Grace talk until they came and told her that she was needed on the floor.

"I'll be back," she told Grace. "I'll look at your chart and we will talk some more."

When Jain had time to check the chart, she found that Grace was going to be one of the lucky ones. Her surgery was scheduled for eight am the next day. If she were lucky enough, she wouldn't even need a colostomy. The biggest risk would be her bad heart, but for now, everything looked pretty good. Her EKG and lab work looked good. When Jain got a few extra minutes, she went and explained everything to Grace in the plain old hillbilly language that they were both familiar with.

"I bet you won't even be here tomorrow." Grace thew this at her as she got to the door, but Jain was prepared.

She turned and leaned on the door facing. "Dana is working days tomorrow. This is Monday and I'm not off 'till Saturday. We've got you covered, Grace." She was rewarded with a weak, toothless smile.

After Dana gave report the next evening, she said; "I'm warning you, Jain, you're in for it. That pain med. has got Grace so confused. The only names she knows are yours and mine. She hit her arm on the side rail and tore the skin. The doctor asked her who let that happen and she told him that you did. No matter what you ask her, she says you did it. I wouldn't want to be in your shoes tonight."

Later that evening when Jain called the doctor to see about getting Grace's med. changed or decreased, he chewed her out for letting Grace get a skin tear. He changed the medication, then hung up on her. The next evening, Grace was back to normal. She was holding onto Jain's hand and talking about Freddie when the doctor came in to check on her.

"I thought you were mad at Jain."

"I wasn't mad at Jain," Grace looked puzzled. "Jain and Dana are the only good nurses in here."

"Is that right?" He tried to hide a smile and went to the nurse's station to write orders. Jain followed.

"You know, yesterday, everything that went wrong, she said you did it. Her IV came out last night and they had to call me out because they couldn't start it back. She had all these blue spots from where they had tried. I asked her who did that to her and she said that you did. She even blamed you for all the world problems."

Grace continued to improve. They kept her in the hospital longer because she was high risk, but she was doing well. Friday finally rolled around. It was day thirteen that Jain had worked without a day off. By some miracle, it was a quiet night. The evening shift personnel were planning a birthday dinner for one of the LPNs for the next night.

Grace stood in the door of her room, listening to the plans. Jain looked at the deep-set wrinkles in her face, at the toothless grin, and the gleam that was now back in her eyes. Sometimes it felt good to be a nurse. Sometimes she thought she actually could make a difference. She smiled as she went about her work

"What are you bringing to the dinner tomorrow, Jain?"

Jain was approaching the station with an IV pole that she had dc'd from a patient down the hall. "I won't be here. It's my night off and I'm going dancing. I'm going to forget it all. This is thirteen nights straight that I've worked." She was almost even with Grace, as she uttered these words.

"Yeah! You'll be dancing all right. You'll be out here dancing up and down these halls with them IV poles." Grace's remark made everyone laugh.

Jain's life was going pretty good. The kids were involved in softball, and baseball. They went to the park to practice after school. One of the LPNs would volunteer to go pick them up and bring them to the hospital where they would stay in an empty room until Jain's shift was over. Jain couldn't leave the hospital because she was the only RN in the building. The children joked that if they saw someone dressed in white drive up in a car, they knew that they were to go and get in. They hated staying at the hospital. Both vowed that they would never be a doctor or a nurse.

Jain felt good about being a nurse most of the time, but at home, at night when she was alone, and the kids were asleep in their beds, she could still hear Ray saying, "You're a nothing, Jain, a nothing and a nobody." No matter what she accomplished, it was always with her. She still felt like a failure. She now hid it well, but there was still nights when she cried herself to sleep. If someone told her that she needed to be married or that she needed a man in her life, she would simply ask, "Why?"

It no longer shattered her world to see Ray and Roni together, or to here someone talk about them. Once in a while he still came by to see the children. He still hadn't paid a dime in child support. It might be a year between visits. He was a stranger to his own kids. It seemed so sad, but at least it was less painful. Brenda still made jokes about Roni being so clumsy and getting hurt so much. It was rumored that Roni had boyfriend. When she was alone and being honest, Jain knew that she still hadn't forgiven Ray. She had such bitterness in her heart when she thought about him, especially when she thought about how he had hurt her children. It ate at her soul. She was still missing part of her life. She still felt incomplete.

Saturday night came, and Jain was feeling depressed. She let the children go stay all night with her sister. They were going to the movies. Jain knew that they wouldn't want to come home before Sunday night. She no longer felt like dancing. She planned on taking a long hot bath, taking the phone off the hook, turning all the lights out and hiding from the world. She lay stretched out on the sofa in her flannel gown and robe with the sad country songs playing on the radio. She felt herself drifting off to sleep.

All of a sudden, there was a pounding on the door. "Oh no," she groaned. It could only be Ray, ready for another fight or else the police, coming to tell her that she was needed at work. She hoped that it was Ray. She actually thought she might just hit him with the kids' bat and slam the door and go to sleep. The pounding continued and she got up and went to the door. When she opened the door, Lucy flipped on the light.

"What are you doing?"

"Nothing, I'm staying home and sleeping all weekend."

"Oh no you're not! Get dressed! You're coming with us. I saw the kids up town. They told me they were spending the weekend with Brenda. I might have known that you'd try something like this."

"What are you doing over here anyway?"

"We've been to see Frank's sister. We have to pass through here to go there. It's a good thing, from the looks of it."

Jain laughed. It was impossible to stay sad around Lucy. "Ok, I'll get dressed and if the car will start, I'll meet you at the dance."

"Oh no you don't! I know you; you'll back out. You get ready and go with us. I'll bring you back after the dance if you won't spend the night with us."

Jain agreed. When they arrived, they were late and all the good seats were taken. They had to sit near the entrance. Jain was closest to the door. The band started playing the square dance music. Someone came through the door and grabbed Jain by the hand, pulling her up and onto the dance floor. As they joined the people forming the circle on the floor, he smiled down at her. "Hello, darlin', "he said as he swung her around and they started the set.

She had been dancing with him the last couple of months when she was there. She knew that he was divorced. His name was Brad and Jain really liked him. He was about six feet tall, had dark brown hair and blue eyes. Her mom didn't like him, but Lucy did.

Lucy told Jain that he often stayed only a little while and left if Jain wasn't there. When the music stopped, he still held her hand. Jain started toward her chair, but he pulled her back to his side. The music started again, this time a slow tune, and they started to dance.

"Where are your kids?"

"Spending the night with my sister."

He held her closer. Her heart beat faster and her knees grew weak as they swayed to the slow beat of the music. They didn't sit down between songs, just stood there and waited for the next. When the band took a break, he walked her outside to a deserted spot, and kissed her. It had been so long, she didn't trust herself to speak. He leaned up against his pickup and kept his arm around her. She didn't want the night to end. She dreaded going home to her empty house, especially since the kids would not be with her. She didn't want to spend the night with Lucy. When the evening ended, she decided home was the only place that she could be.

"Why don't you spend the night with me?" Lucy asked. "I'll take you home in the morning. It's late and you will be by yourself."

"I'll take you home. I'm not tired. I really had a good time tonight." Jain hadn't seen Brad walk up. "I don't want the night to end."

With his arm around her, it was hard to say no and Lucy was all for it. Jain suspected that she'd been set up, but Lucy later denied this.

Brad did take her home, and he spent the night. He was tender and loving, and Jain had not been able to resist him. That night, she hadn't wanted to, but the next day, after he had gone, she was a mess. She felt dirty. She called herself all the names that she had ever heard. She had done the things that she had sworn she never would. She was ashamed of herself. She couldn't look at the picture of Jesus that hung on her wall. She couldn't listen to the preachers on TV. She paced the floor. She called the kids, but they didn't want to come home. They were going fishing with Brenda and her family. They would be home at bedtime. Jain sank deeper into despair. When the phone rang, she didn't answer. She felt more isolated and alone than ever, and when she cried out to God, she didn't think that He heard her. She pulled herself together the next morning only because she had to. She got the kids off to school, then later in the day, she went to work.

It was like she was a different person when she was working.

She stopped going to the dance. The children still went once in awhile, with Brenda or their grandmother, but Jain would not go. Brad called a few times, but she had the kids to tell him that she wasn't home. She walked around with her head hung down. For the first time in her life, she really believed that Ray had been right. She was worse than a nothing. She really was a nobody. She kept all this inside. She was more adept now, at hiding her feelings. She prayed that God wouldn't hold her sins against her children. She prayed that He would still protect and shelter them in spite of her shortcomings. Although she still felt estranged from God, she thought that those prayers were answered, because the children continued to thrive. She had heard somewhere that the word life meant constant change and she believed it to be true. Nothing ever stayed the same for her. It seemed like something changed every time she turned around.

This time the change was good. Her schedule had been changed. Now she worked part time on days and part time on evenings. Once in awhile, she got called in on midnights. It was not an easy schedule to get used to, but she had more time with the children. She hoped some how to get to work straight days. It wasn't likely to happen because there was always a shortage of nurses. She had to admit that she liked the variety of the different shifts and getting to work with the people that she used to work with again. They said that they missed her and always seemed glad to have her for charge nurse. Sometimes she pulled a double shift. This week, she had worked days on Monday and Tuesday and was scheduled for evenings on Friday, Saturday, and Sunday.

On Friday she went to report. Dana said; "In room 101 is Roni Davis. She fell off the ladder when she was helping her husband fix the porch. She has three fractured ribs and has developed pneumonia. Her temp is 101.6. She's congested and complains of pain everytime she moves. Her IV is 60 cc/hr and she gets ampicillin 500 mg IVPB q 8 hrs. She needs to turn, cough, and deep breath q 2, and get her up in a chair if you can." No one seemed to make the connection between Roni and Jain.

Dana finished report and Jain made assignments. She gave Roni to the most experienced LPN so that she wouldn't have to go into the room. She didn't think Roni would want her there. Roni's room was close to the nurses' station. She was one of the sicker patients tonight and they usually put the sickest patients nearest to the station. The door to her room was open, and Jain noticed that Ray was sitting there, holding Roni's hand. He stayed there until seven, then came to the desk where Jain was charting.

"You'd better not let anything happen to her." He said this low, through gritted teeth. The air was charged with his hatred. The other nurses looked shocked.

"Lisa will take very good care of her." Jain spoke calmly. Ray no longer had the power to frighten or upset her. "We have your phone number. We'll call if she needs you."

Jain noticed from the chart that Roni had tolerated only a few bites of her full liquid diet. She needed to have plenty of fluids. "Maybe she will drink a coke," she told Lisa. "She needs the fluids."

"She won't do anything! That girl has an attitude problem. She won't turn or cough or take a deep breath. She has a foul mouth."

At eight o'clock, when they made their rounds, Lisa came and got Jain. "You're going to have to restart that IV on Roni Davis. I've stuck her three times and I can't get it. She acts like you're killing her if you touch her."

"OK, but you'll have to stay in there with me. She's married to my ex. They might cause trouble and I might need a witness."

They took the IV tray to Roni's room. Jain saw the look of fear on Roni's face as she entered and she was sure that Roni saw the shock on hers. Roni had more than broken ribs and pneumonia. She had a black eye and a swollen lip. Jain was not at all sure her injuries were due to a fall. Defiance and a sneer soon replaced the look of fear on her face.

Jain approached the bed. "Roni, we have to restart your IV. You need the fluids and the antibiotics. It's time to hang your ampicillin now. If you can hold still, it will only take a moment to restart you, then it won't hurt. You talk to Lisa while I get it going." She applied the tourniquet, swabbed the arm, and slid the 20-gauge angiocath into the vein. She connected the tubing, removed the tourniquet, and adjusted the rate. As she taped the small dressing and tubing in place, she said; "If you'll drink more liquids, your temp will go down faster. It will be easier to cough up the mucus and you'll get rid of the IV faster."

As Jain went to the sink to wash her hands, she heard Roni mutter a foul word under her breath. She's still just a child, Jain thought. A brat for sure, but just a child. If she were my child, I might be tempted to spank her, or apply a little of this soap and water to her mouth, but even Roni doesn't deserve what she's been through.

Back at the nurses' station, Jain asked Lisa; "Will she talk to you? Did she really fall, or do you think she's been beaten?"

"I'd like to beat her." This was uncharacteristic of Lisa. She usually had tons of compassion.

"I know how she is. I'll give her to someone else tomorrow, but see what you can do for her tonight. Ray abused me, and he might be doing the same thing to her."

When Jain gathered information for report, she found that Roni had drank a coke and that her temp was down to 99.6 and the IV was fine. The next day, she was even better and Ray was demanding that she be sent home. Jain wouldn't call the doctor to get a discharge order because he had already checked on Roni earlier and thought she needed to stay at least one more day. She tried to explain this to Ray as he stood at the nurses' station and raged. In the end, he kicked a stool over and stormed out. At the end of her shift, when she started to go give report to the midnight shift, she stuck her head in Roni's room. She knew better, but she had to try.

"Roni, is everything all right at home? Do you need to talk to someone?"

"It's none of your business! Butt out! Get a life and stay out of ours!" Roni threw the water pitcher and it hit the wall next to the door.

Jain collected the children. They barely woke up enough to get into and out of the car, and slept through the night and into the next day. Jain couldn't sleep. She was restless. She didn't know why she even cared. She and the kids were safe enough. They were out of it. She was grateful for that. She didn't know who was taking care of Ray and Roni's child. She didn't know what she could do about it anyway. Roni was right about one thing. It was none of her business. Still, she had a bad feeling that something was not right. Something was going to happen. She got out of bed and got down on her knees and prayed. She still felt that God was a long way from her, but maybe not as distant as he had been for awhile.

The next day when she got to work, Roni was gone and she couldn't help but be glad. She pushed the incident to the back of her mind. She bought five acres of land and started planning to build a home for herself and the kids.

Chapter 5

They were no longer starving, but they were still living from paycheck to paycheck. Rent took a big hunk of that paycheck. Jain dreamed of owning her own home and was glad that she had finally managed to save a down payment on five acres of land. She would have to make payments for a year, but then it would belong to her and the kids. They would finally have a real home. When the land was paid off, they would build a house. She would do it a little at a time. She would not mortgage her land. She wanted her kids to have roots, a place where they belonged.

On the day that she closed the deal, she and the kids walked all around the property. About half of the land was level and cleared, but the other half was woods, hills, and hollers. It was located only three miles from town and only one mile from her sister's house. It was early fall, not really cold, but a light rain was falling. They were bundled into jeans and coats with hoods, laughing and talking about the kind of house they'd build. Walking single file, with Jain in the lead, they walked the entire parameter of the land. The kids laughed each time that she stumbled or slipped on the wet leaves. They teased her about being old. Looking over her shoulder, she teased them back.

As they neared the end of the walk and topped the hill, Jain tripped on a vine and fell to the ground. Her left arm warped a tree. Just for a second, she thought she was going to pass out. She felt a searing, sharp pain shoot through her arm, then a frightening numbness, along with a sick feeling. Then there was throbbing pain. Jain knew that her arm was broken. For a moment, she couldn't speak or move. Panic threatened to overwhelm her.

"Mom! Mom! Are you alright?"

Both kids had converged on her. She saw the fear in their eyes and summoned every ounce of courage that she could find.

"I think I broke my arm." She had to stay calm for the children's sake. "I need a little help."

They helped her to the car. Thank God for automatic transmissions. She drove to Brenda's house. Brenda took her to the clinic. They x-rayed her arm, gave her some pain medication, put her arm in a splint and a sling, and sent her home. She was quiet. Her arm now had a continuous, throbbing pain. It was swollen too much to put on a cast. She wondered how she was going to manage now, then she remembered that she had vacation time and sick days that she could take. She breathed a sigh of relief.

"You'd better be careful" Brenda joked. "They'll start calling you Roni. I heard that she had a fight with a ladder. Did you have to be her nurse?"

"No. Listen, Brenda, I'm not so sure about all those accidents. You know how Ray treated me. I have a bad feeling about them."

"Jain! Don't tell me that you feel sorry for her. After all that she put you through, how could you care what happens to her?"

"I don't know, it's not like I love her or anything—- it's just that I have a sense of foreboding, a really bad feeling when I think about it. Something bad will happen."

"You have got to be crazy. If he is being mean to her, she asked for it. Besides, I heard that he's driving a truck now. He's gone most of the time. That ought to make her happy." Brenda changed the subject as they pulled into the drive, but Jain knew what she meant. It seemed that everyone except Ray knew about Roni's boyfriend.

"Mom! I was afraid they'd keep you in the hospital!" Stan wrapped his arms around her legs. Cass gave him a disgusted look.

"No, not for a broken arm, but I'll have to take some vacation days. I can't work for awhile." Thank God that I have vacation days, she thought.

In spite of everything, she was slowly making a better life for herself and the kids. Ray's life didn't seem to be going so well. Sometimes she almost felt sorry for him, but then she would think of all that she and the children had suffered because of him and she would think that he was only getting what he deserved. Her feelings were just as mixed about Roni. She wondered why she cared. Brenda definitely had a point. Roni had caused a world of grief and misery for Jain and the kids. Still, they would be all right; they were better off without Ray than they had ever been with him.

A week later, the swelling went down and they put a cast on her arm. It helped, but she was still handicapped. The children helped a lot. We've become a close-nit family, Jain thought. We really count on each other and pull together in hard times. She really enjoyed the time with the kids. In spite of all the hard times, or maybe because of them, they made a great team. If one was sick or hurt, the other two were right there to help. The never doubted that they'd get through a crisis. Jain was amazed at her children and so very thankful for them. Ray could keep his money. She had the kids.

Two weeks later, she went back to work. Since she was right handed, she could sign off orders and be charge nurse. There was always such a shortage of RN's. She had to delegate more work to the others, but they gave her an extra person to help. It was the easiest four weeks she'd ever spent at work. She had more time to talk with the patients and her peers. Sometimes the talk was serious. They shared their deepest feelings.

Some of the nurses believed that God, to a certain extent, protected nurses from disease. They worked around all kinds of infectious diseases and didn't get sick. Sure, they knew that it was partly due to good handwashing, reverse isolation and the other policies and procedures that they used to keep down infections, but they had more immunity to disease than most people did. Jain believed this. She knew for sure that she would have never been a nurse without God's help. Looking back, she wondered how she'd ever made it. She knew that she hadn't done it alone.

Her next weekend off dawned warm and sunny. Some called it Indian Summer. It was a beautiful time of the year, but you could never be sure how long it would last. Jain felt wonderful! Her arm wasn't hurting. The cast had been trimmed and she had better use of her left hand. She woke the kids at seven am, determined not to waste the day.

"Get up! It's a beautiful day. We'll go shopping, get those new jeans that you've been wanting. We can get hamburgers for lunch, then see a movie. We'll make a day of it." She already had breakfast on the table.

Stan stumbled into the kitchen, rubbing the sleep from his eyes. Cass was just behind him, looking like she wasn't sure if this was a good idea or not. Something about the sun shinning through the kitchen window, the food on the table, and their mother's smile made the happiness contagious. Soon the children were just as excited about the trip as their mother. They ate and dressed, then piled into the car. They played 'I Spy' and knock-knock jokes as Jain drove the forty miles to the mall. The first thing they bought was the blue jeans, two pair for each child, then they checked out the sales. Stan wasn't happy about that, but Jain bribed him to be good by promising to give him some money and let him go to the toy store later. Cass had a ball. The budget was shot, but Jain didn't care. She could cut back on a few other things. This was going to be a wonderful day. She wouldn't let anything spoil it. When the shopping was done, they locked all the bags into the trunk of the car, and went back into the mall.

Jain gave the kids five dollars each, and let them go into the toy store while she sat on a bench at the entrance. She knew they'd look at everything before they decided what to buy. She wasn't surprised, when thirty minutes later, Stan came running out.

"Mom! I need two more dollars and so does Cass. We found what we want, but we don't have enough money."

Jain gave them the money. She'd been expecting this. She told them to hurry, they had to get the movie tickets and eat lunch. To her surprise, they were at her side with their purchases in less than ten minutes. They went to the theater to get the tickets. The movie that they wanted to see wouldn't start for an hour, so they went to eat lunch. They gobbled down hamburgers, fries and milk shakes, all the fatty foods that Jain knew they shouldn't have, but she couldn't refuse them once in a while. They got back to the theater with time to spare.

Another movie was letting out. Jain stirred the kids around the mob of people that was pouring out onto the sidewalk, content with the world, feeling happy and peaceful. This feeling was shattered abruptly as she heard the angry, sneering voice of Roni. She and Ray were coming out of the theater.

"We can't go anywhere without seeing her! She has to ruin everything."

Jain looked up and into Roni's thunderous gaze. Ray also looked up and Jain saw his facial features change into hardness. The air felt charged with his hatred. His fists clenched at his sides. The children crowded closer to Jain's sides. For a moment, it seemed that they were frozen in time, as people continued to move around them, then Jain gently pushed the kids forward.

"Come on," she told them, "We're going to be late for the movie." She moved behind them on shaky legs. She could still hear Ray and Roni. She looked back. Roni was pouting and Ray had his arm around her.

"I'll talk to her. I'll make sure she stays out of our way. Just forget about her, Baby. Let's enjoy the weekend. I have to leave on a three-day trip on Monday."

Jain knew right then that she was in for it. She could feel the trouble coming. It seemed that every time Ray and Roni had trouble, they blamed it on her.

That was the only time he ever came around. He had always had a temper, but it seemed to be getting worse. Jain thought about the fights that they'd had when they were married. It had been bad, but nothing like the ones he and Roni had, if that was the cause of Roni's condition when she was in the hospital. Jain was afraid of Ray now. It was hard to believe that she had once loved him more than she loved her own life. Now she prayed for him to stay away from her and the kids as hard as she had once prayed for him to come home. He didn't.

Sunday morning, before daylight, she heard the pounding on the door. She thought about not answering it, but that wouldn't work. The kids would wake up and let him in, or he would break her door in. She rolled out of bed and grabbed her robe. As soon as she turned the lock, he shoved the door open.

"Why do you have to ruin my life? Why can't you leave me alone? I'm so sick and tired of you. I ought to have you killed. I know people who would do it Jain. They'd do it in a minute. You are pushing your luck. Roni is my life. You are nothing."

Jain had backed up to the phone while Ray raged, and she held the receiver in her hand. As he stepped inside with his fist clenched, she dialed 911. She knew better than to say family disturbance.

"There's an intruder in my house." She said this as Ray's fist slammed the wall, knocking a picture off the wall and shattering the glass. She gave her address.

She knew the police would come, that the address would be familiar. For once, she was glad that they had been sent to get her to go to work so often. They wouldn't think of her connection to Ray. He must have known it too, because Jain could see him fighting to gain self-control. She prayed the children would stay in their beds, she knew that they couldn't still be asleep. Five minutes later, the police cruiser pulled into the drive and the officer got out. Jain's hopes were dashed.

"Hey! Ray, old buddy. What's going on? We got a call about an intruder."

"Just a little family problem, nothing to worry about. I was just leaving. See you buddy." Ray slapped the officer on the shoulder, got into his car, and drove away.

Jain stepped onto the porch. "It was not a family dispute. We have been divorced for a long time. He can't come over here and cause trouble. He knocked a hole in the wall and broke that picture frame. He was going to hit me. My children will be frightened. This has got to stop."

"Now, Jain. It's only Ray. You know he wouldn't hurt you. He's got a little temper, but there's no harm in him. If he gives you anymore trouble, I'll talk to him." The officer, who was Ray's friend Bill, got in his car and left.

Jain was furious. She paced the floor and cried. They were tears of anger, not pain. She was too mad to be frightened. She didn't know which one she was the angriest at, Bill or Ray. She wanted to move; to get out of this town; away from Ray and his friends, but every time that she talked about moving away, the kids got upset. They didn't want to leave their family and friends. She thought about doing it anyway, but then she thought about how much they'd already lost. She sat on the sofa and cried harder.

"Mom, are you alright?" Stan put his hand on her shoulder.

She stopped crying, wiped her eyes, and blew her nose. “Yes, baby, I’m alright.”

She knew that he didn’t want her to call him baby, but she couldn’t seem to help it. They would always be her babies, no matter how old they were. She loved them so much and she felt like she had failed them in so many ways.

Stan was bare footed and Cass was coming into the room. She had to pull herself together. Yesterday she had been so happy. Now she was feeling the depths of despair. She looked at her children and knew that she had to go on. She tried to smile.

“Watch out. Don’t step on the glass. You’ll cut your feet.”

They didn’t ask what had happened. Jain knew that they’d heard it all, probably been looking out the window at Ray and Bill. As she cleaned up the mess, she thought once again that she hated Ray and Roni and their friends. It gnawed at her. It made her body tense. It just ate away at her. She couldn't help it. She didn't care if Ray did beat Roni! She wished he'd beat old buddy, Bill a few times! She resented the fact that she couldn't even take her kids to the movies in peace. Why was Roni still stirring up trouble? She had Ray. What more did she want? Jain for sure didn't want him back. She'd be happy to never lay eyes on him again.

It was the tone of his voice, not the words that Stan was speaking that snapped her out of her thoughts.

"What did you say?"

"I said that when I'm big enough, I'm going to beat Ray until he can't get up. He's going to be sorry for making you cry."

For a minute, she couldn't speak. She didn't know what to say. Then she gathered her son into her arms and reached for her daughter.

It's ok," she told them, "Ray didn't hurt me. He just had a temper tantrum, like a small child that doesn't get it's way. Now I'm acting like a baby. No wonder you guys don't want me to call you baby. Lets fix breakfast and see what we are going to do today. If it's still warm enough, we might go all the way down to the Tennessee River, that little park that you like, and have a picnic."

When they got to the park and things were calm, she tried to explain to her son that beating people up wasn't the way to resolve problems. It was easier to have the serious talks there by the river with the blanket spread and the blue water flowing peacefully on. There were few boats on the water, and few people in the park, but it was just what they needed to soothe and heal them. By Monday the were ready to go back to school and work, but Jain wondered how long would their peace last this time.

Why won't Ray and Roni just leave us alone? He doesn't even pay child support and he doesn't even see the children when he comes around. I can sort of understand her behavior when I was married to Ray. She wanted him and she wanted to break us up, but now she has him. They are married and have a child. I sure don't want him back. I don't bother them. We don't even have the same friends anymore, yet they keep on causing problems. Our lives should be separate. I know I'm the one they want to hurt, but they are hurting my children. Oh God, I wish they'd just go away. All these thoughts raced through Jain's mind as she got the kids ready for school and herself ready for work. She knew from past experience, that it could be months or just weeks before she would have any further contact with Ray. She remembered hearing him tell Roni that he would be gone for three days on the truck. She was glad. She wished he would never come back. She wished he and Roni would move to a different state and she'd never have to see either of them again.

She got to work early, entering the hospital from the employee entrance. She'd stop in the dinning room for another cup of coffee. As she neared the door, she almost bumped into 'good buddy, Bill', coming out with a steaming cup.

"Hey, Jain! Well, Old Ray left out early. I saw him about five this morning, filling up his rig. He wanted me to come by and check on Roni. She got up in the dark and fell down the stairs. She's pretty banged up. I swear, that girl is clumsy. See ya." He went out the rear entrance, as Jain stood there with her mouth open.

Jain was dumbfounded. Could Bill really be that ignorant? He was a policeman for goodness sake. Then she remembered how blind she had been when she was Ray's wife, and how stupid everyone had thought her to be. If love was blind, she guessed that friendship could be also. She felt kinder toward Bill, but in her heart, she thought that those 'stairs' that Roni had fallen down, were the ones that Ray had planned to give to her. When they were married, he had abused her, but not to this extent. He was getting worse, or he was more confident of getting away with it. But what could she do? Why did she care? By now, especially after this past weekend, she agreed with Brenda. Roni deserved it. All she wanted was for them to leave her and the kids alone.

Who was she kidding? No one deserved it, and where was the little girl when all this was going on? Jain thought that Roni's parents kept her most of the time, but she wasn't sure. If she was charge nurse today, she was going to see about getting a social services eval for Roni. It might not help, but at least she'd know she'd tried. She might be making things worse, but they didn't leave her alone anyway. She was tired of it all. The others started arriving for report, and Jain finished her coffee. It looked like a busy day.

Jain talked to the doctor and got an order for a social service eval on Roni. He was a little reluctant, but when he reviewed the number of times she'd been treated for accidents, he decided that it might be justified. The social worker made her visit that very day. Roni was furious, but Jain was shocked. After the visit, Mrs. Hunter came to the nurses' station to talk to Jain.

"Is there some place where we could talk in private?"

They used the empty doctors' lounge.

"Jain, have you ever thought about getting counseling? Roni seems to think that you can't let go of Ray. She says that they wouldn't have problems if you would only leave them alone."

"What? I don't bother them! I don't even make Ray pay child support! They are the ones who won't leave me alone. It's Ray who keeps coming to my house and putting his fist through the wall and Roni who drives by yelling obscenities from her car window." Jain took a deep breath and tried to calm down. "Look, I'm a nurse. Roni has been in the hospital several times with bruises from head to toe. I didn't give them to her. It's my job to help her if I can. I have done my part."

"Jain," Mrs. Hunter tried again. "I know it must be hard to see the man that you love with someone else. I know it would be for me. Maybe it would help to talk to someone. Here's my card. If you don't want to talk to me, the office could recommend someone else. Just think about it. Even nurses need help sometimes."

"Look, Mrs. Hunter, the divorce was years ago. I've made a new life for myself and for my kids. The last thing I want is to talk about the past. I feel that Roni and Ray need help. I don't know how this got to be about me. I don't have the bruises."

Jain saw the pity in Mrs. Hunter's eyes and knew that her efforts were futile. She smiled and extended her hand. "If you'll excuse me, I have to get back to work. I hope that you left your card with Roni."

"How did it go?"

Lisa looked hopeful. Poor Lisa. She seemed to get stuck with caring for Roni most of the time. Jain hated to disappoint her.

"Mrs. Hunter thinks that I need to be counseled. Roni told her that I was the cause of all her Problems."

"You're kidding!"

"No, honest! She thinks that I can't let go of Ray, even though the divorce was years ago and Roni and Ray have been married for years and have a child. She left me her card. I hope that she left Roni one."

"I wish that she had to take care of Roni for a few days! I get so aggravated at her, then I feel so sorry for her. One minute she is screaming obscenities and the next, she is lying there with those big, silent tears on her cheeks."

"I know, but I've done all that I know to do. My sister thinks that I'm crazy for worrying about it. The social worker thinks I want Ray back. He will be on a rampage when he gets back in town, but I'm not taking any more of his abuse. I don't know how to stop him, but there must be a way."

Jain was glad this day was over. She kept thinking about what the social worker had said. It made her mad; then she would think that it was funny. It was amazing how many people thought that she wanted Ray back. She knew that they thought that because she didn't have a man in her life. No way would she have him back.

When the children went to bed, she went through the house locking all the doors and windows. Sometimes, she caught herself double checking the locks. She didn't used to be so cautious. It hit her then;

She wasn't really free after all. She still lived in fear: Fear that Ray would be back; that he would break into her house; that he would hurt the children. She lay in bed, thinking about everything. Maybe she should try dating again. Ray would stay away if he thought there was a man around, but she wasn't ready for that.

When Ray was happy, he left her alone. Every time that he had a problem, he blamed it on Jain. It seemed that if he was unhappy, Jain paid. Would she never be free of him? She longed for peace. She prayed that she'd live long enough to get her children grown. If something happened to her, Ray might get custody of the children, even though she knew that he didn't want them. It made her almost hysterical to think of the life that they'd have if that happened.

This was the first time that she'd feared for her life since she worked at the restaurant and that man had followed her home. Now, she didn't even have her sister's dog for protection. A dog! She'd get one. It would make the children happy and make her home more safe. She would start looking for one tomorrow.

The next day, things were a little better. Roni was discharged from the hospital. As she was wheeled past Jain in the hall, she said, "You are going to be real sorry for this. Ray will be home in two more days."

"That will be your problem, not mine." Jain did not feel a bit objective nor like a professional at the moment. She was tired of it all. At the moment, she didn't care if Ray did beat Roni, but he was going to leave her and the children alone. She asked her co-workers if they knew where she might get a good guard dog. No one did. They thought that she should get a restraining order instead. Jain knew from experience that didn't work. It was useless to tell them that she'd tried that before.

When she got home, she told the kids that Ray would be back in town in two days. They were quiet. She told them that they were going to get a dog. That made them happy. She enlisted their help to nail boards on the windows from the inside of the house and to add extra locks to the doors. When the children went to bed, she called Lucy. She had to talk to someone. Lucy would fuss and make radical suggestions, but she would listen and she would care.

This time, Lucy really helped. She knew where Jain could get a dog.

"Listen, Jain, I don't know about this dog. It belongs to my aunt. She wants to give it away because she wants to travel. It likes women and children ok, but it tried to bite Frank. It's half Doberman."

"Sounds like it's just what I need. Listen, Lucy, Ray is getting worse. I've thought about moving away, but if I did, he'd just find me. The children don't want to move away from their grandmother and their aunts. I have to stand up to him, make him see that he can't treat us this way."

"I'll call my aunt. You can come over here tomorrow when you get home from work and we'll go see the dog. I still don't think it's a good idea. You know I don't like dogs."

It was love at first site between the kids and the dog. The dog wiggled all over and wagged its stub of a tail as it accepted hugs and pats from the kids. Its name was Jill; odd name for a dog, but it seemed to fit. They took it home that very night, and Jain continued to think about ways to make improvements. Things were going to change. She knew that she couldn't count on the police or social services, or anyone else. She wasn't bitter. She knew that some people cared and would help if they knew how, but they couldn't. That night, she knelt at her bedside and poured her heart out to God.

Chapter 6

Fear kept her in a constant state of alertness. It wasn't a cowering kind of fear. She didn't go around saying, "What will I do?" and wringing her hands, but she was always tense; always watchful. She found herself listening for the sound of Ray's car in the drive. She awoke if the children made the slightest sound. Her co-workers called her paranoid. The children started teasing her about how good she could hear.

"Be quiet! Mom can hear the grass grow!" They'd tell their friends.

Jill lived in the house. Jain made the children wake her before the let the dog go outside. She feared that Ray would harm the children just to hurt her. A strange car had been driving by her house two or three times a day. It drove by slowly and the man was always looking at the house. The front yard was small and when the children were outside, they were usually in the back. Jain hated that they also lived with fear, but was glad that they were wary of strangers. The dog didn't like strangers either, so they had fenced in the back yard. Jain was still thinking of ways to keep them safe. She was thankful for close neighbors, even though she dreamed of getting her house built and moving in. She stood in her front yard, talking to her neighbor and listening to the children and the dog playing out back. They watched as the strange car crept slowly up the street.

"Who on earth is that?" her neighbor asked. "He makes me feel uneasy. I called the police, but they didn't do anything."

"I know what you mean. I've been watching him too. I've never seen him around before this week. He gives me the creeps."

They watched the car go out of sight, but couldn't read the tag number for the mud splattered on it. Jain kept the baseball bat by the door these days.

About midnight, Jain was awakened by an unfamiliar sound. At first, she didn't recognize it. It grew louder and more menacing. As she became fully awake, she realized that Jill was at the foot of her bed growling, every hair turned the wrong way. For a moment, Jain was frozen, and then she heard the front window rattle. She eased out of bed and checked on the children. They were sound asleep. She checked all the locks. Jill sounded more viscous with each passing second, and Jain went to her side, bat in hand. She stroked the dog's head, but it ignored her. Jain grabbed the flashlight from the nightstand and crept quietly to the window, Jill at her side. It was dark, but she could see the shape of a person, pulling at the bottom of the window. She shined the light through the crack in the boards that she had nailed up. By sheer luck, it shown directly into the person's eyes. Who ever it was fell backward, muttered a profanity, then ran toward the street. Minutes later, Jain heard a car roar away. Jill became calm and Jain started shaking. She checked the children again. They were still sleeping, but Jain didn't even go back to bed. Jill slept on the couch with her head in Jain's lap.

At the first light of day, Jain checked outside. At the front window of her bedroom, she found a crowbar and saw the damage at the bottom of the window, where someone had tried to pry it open. She realized that they were trying to sneak in, otherwise, they would have just broken the glass. She reported it to the police, but she knew that it was useless. They called it an attempted robbery and somehow, it was printed in the weekly newspaper but Jain knew better. Nothing was mentioned about the dog, and Jain was glad. Jill would be a nice surprise for Ray. He had to be behind this; it had to be him- - - Or Roni. Whoever had done it had known where her bedroom was located. They must have known that she was home, because her car had been parked out front. She remembered Ray's rage, and Roni saying, "You'll pay for this. Ray will be home in two days"

Ray showed up the next day. The children weren't home, and she saw him when he pulled into the drive. She left Jill inside and met him in the front yard. It was safer.

"The kids aren't home today. You'll have to see them some other time."

"I didn't come to see them! You've done it this time, Jain! I told you to leave Roni alone! Social Services! How dare you but into our business. Roni said that Mrs. Hunter could see right through you and didn't believe a word that you said. She's been coming by two or three times a week, just to make sure that you are not harassing us. She was there this morning when I got in. I told her I'd take care of it." He took a step closer, fists clenched.

Jain noticed that they were attracting attention from the neighbors. They had inched closer. Ray hadn't noticed.

"I'd have been here sooner if my rig hadn't broken down out in Texas." He took a deep breath, then continued. "I'm here now, and I won't have you upsetting my wife."

"Look, Ray, I was only trying to help. I really want you and Roni to make it. All I want is for you to leave me alone. I am not going to take any more abuse from either one of you. Those days are over. Get it through your head. I'm also not going to drop off the face of the earth."

He looked like he was about to explode. He swung his fist, but she dodged and he missed by an inch. Her neighbor ran to her side, his wife behind him, and Ray stomped away. His tires peppered them with gravel as he peeled out of her drive. "Thank God the kids weren't home." She didn't realize that she had spoken her thought until her neighbors agreed. She went inside and tried to calm down.

As she sat on the sofa, sipping her tea and stroking Jill's head, it hit her. Ray just got back in town. It couldn't have been him who tried to break into her house. Who then? She had been so sure that it was Ray and that he wanted to frighten her. She dropped her cup. She was more afraid than ever. Roni had been at her house before, left her notes in the mailbox and harassed her, but nothing like this. Where do I go for help? No one takes it seriously. They consider it family trouble. These thoughts ran through her mind, but she had no answers. She stepped up safety measures once again. She let the children spend more time with her family, thinking that they were safer there. She tried to stay busy enough to keep from thinking, especially now, when the kids were spending the night with their grandmother. It didn't always work.

Exhaustion caught up with her and she slept like the dead. She awoke at ten the next morning and went to the kitchen for a cup of coffee, only to find that she was out. Oh well, she'd run to the grocery store, get groceries, come home and have her coffee and breakfast, then go get the kids. She was starving. She didn't remember eating at all yesterday. She threw on jeans and a tee shirt and headed out. She was about to turn into the parking lot of the nearest grocery store, when she saw Ray and Roni, his arm around her shoulders, going in the door. It wasn't worth it. She drove on. She'd shop at the higher priced store. Maybe she could avoid Ray and Roni for the rest of her life. That would be great, but she knew it wasn't possible. She hoped that they hadn't seen her. She didn't want to deal with them today. She wasn't a coward; she was just so tired of fighting. She longed for just a few days of peace. She went to get the children. Brenda met her at the door.

"I've got something to tell you! You'll like this Jain. Even you have to think this is funny. Roni's boy friend went to see her early this morning, like he does most mornings when Ray is out of town, and when he knocked, Ray opened the door for him. They said that Ray asked him what he wanted and he was so shocked that he didn't know what to say. He just turned and left."

Jain pictured the scene in her mind, then she started to laugh. She didn't know what else to do. Jain still didn't know who Roni's boyfriend was, but she couldn't help but be curious. How could Ray not know? Then she remembered how blind and ignorant she had been, and she felt sorry for him. How could she have not known?

"Poor Ray."

"For heaven's sakes, Jain! Poor Ray indeed! He's just getting paid back for what he did to you. How can you be so gullible? How can you be so smart in some ways and so stupid in others? No wonder people think you still love him."

"No, Bren, you know I don't. But he's my children's daddy, and people get killed over love triangles. You see it in the news all the time, and I see people come through the emergency room almost every week because of so called 'domestic violence'. It is funny in a way, but it's scary too. Besides, they blame me with all their problems, when they are unhappy, I pay. I still have this awful feeling that something bad is going to happen."

"Oh well, I have some more information, but I don't guess you want to hear it."

"What? I'm sure I will end up being involved in it anyway."

"Roni's boyfriend is married. He has a wife and three kids. He tells his wife that he has to go to work early, and stops by to see Roni. He just didn't know that Ray was home." Brenda laughed. "His wife is a nurse and she works evening shift part time. I don't know her name."

"Does she work at our hospital?"

"I don't know."

Jain had a strange sensation and she suddenly thought of Lisa. No. It couldn't be. Lisa was happily married. No man would want Roni when he had Lisa.

They spent the rest of the day catching up on news of family and friends. Jain told Brenda about her fears, and about her plans to avoid Ray and Roni if she could. They made plans for the house that Jain was going to build. It was already a joke to some folks. They didn't think that she could ever do it. Most thought that she ought to mortgage the land and have a company home built, but she knew that if she did that, she'd have to make payments for the rest of her life. She was determined not to do that. She wanted to have something to leave to her children.

Things settled down and she didn't hear anything more from Ray and Roni. She almost forgot about them. She even forgot to avoid them. Even work was less hectic. Lisa was working more. Jain sometimes stayed over a few minutes just to talk to her. Lisa complained that her husband was working more and more hours and bringing home less money. He kept the kids while she worked, but would take them out riding or out for hamburgers at night. It didn't do her a lot of good to work when he did that. There was never enough money. Jain reminded her that it was still better than having to have a baby sitter. At least they were with their father.

“You’re right. Sometimes they even bring my supper and eat in the cafeteria with me and I get to kiss my kids good night. It could be a lot worse.”

“I can’t believe how well things are going for me right now. I haven’t even seen any strange cars in my neighborhood. I haven’t seen anything of Ray or Roni. I feel like holding my breath or something so it will last.”

"It’s been a long time since Roni has been here. No more accidents. Maybe that social service worker did more good than we thought she did. Maybe Ray and Roni found a way to work out their problems. Oh God I hope so. She is so hard to care for”

"I heard some gossip from Brenda about Roni and her boyfriend."

She didn't get to share the news with Lisa. The ER got busy and Lisa had to get to work. Jain left, collected the kids, and went home. She was restless and so were they. Jill must have had a boring day too, because she wiggled more than usual and her stub of a tail worked overtime when they opened the door. Jain sat down on the sofa, dreading to cook supper. The kids did the same.

"Momma, can we go for hamburgers? It's my night to wash dishes and I don't want to." Cass gave her a soulful look.

"I don't want to cook either. Get in the car. We'll take Jill and she can have a hamburger too."

Jain watched the three of them bounce out the door and into the car, funny how their energy returned so much faster than hers. She took them to the drive in café and they ordered the burgers. Jill attracted attention, sticking her head out the window. A man and three little boys pulled in next to them, and the kids kept pointing excitedly at the dog. The man kept looking around as if he were expecting someone to join them. He wasn't disappointed. To Jain's surprise, Roni sauntered up to his window and kissed him on the lips. His face turned red and he said something to her, then looked toward his children. Roni laughed. She pointed at Jain, said something to the man, then laughed again. The man looked desperate as he gestured with his hands and talked to Roni. They talked for a few more minutes, then Roni pulled her head out of the window and smiled.

"I'll see you when the kids go to sleep."

Then she walked away. She starred at Jain as she passed by and the look on her face said that she meant to cause more trouble.

Jain put the kids to bed and tried to forget about seeing Roni and that man, but she couldn't get Roni's smirk out of her mind. Surely she wouldn't send Ray over this time. She wouldn't tell him that she'd been talking to that man. It almost had to be the boyfriend that Brenda had told her about, but maybe he wasn't. He could have been family. Still, Jain had one of her 'bad feelings'. She could almost feel the trouble in the air. She double-checked all the locks. She was relieved when the next morning at work, she ran into 'Good Buddy Bill' and he told her that Ray's rig was broken down again. He wouldn't be making it home this week. That truck sure did break down a lot to be nearly new. Ray usually was so particular about his vehicles.

When Jain made her rounds, the first room that she entered was 101, where Mrs. Elvia Smith sat propped up in bed. She winced when she coughed. She had three fractured ribs and multiple bruises on her body. The bruises, normally covered by her clothing, were faintly visible through the thin hospital gown. Her face was pale and her eyes were lifeless. Jain remembered the first time that she had met her, in the ER, when she'd been in that car wreck. No car wreck this time: A door had hit her. The 'door' must have really went wild, for she had two broken ribs on the left side and one on the right. It had also put bruises on the front and on the back of her body. Jain just had to try one more time to reach her. She sat in the chair by her bed.

"Mrs. Smith, do you feel like talking about how you got hurt?"

"No."

Jain tried to think of some open ended questions, anything that Mrs. Smith couldn't answer with a yes or no. She was not successful. Finally, she gave up and finished her rounds, but her frustration still showed when she got back to the nurse's station. The doctor was writing orders.

"Okay, Jain. What is it?"

"I think that Mrs. Smith's 'door' has two large fists."

"You could be right. We can give Mrs. Hunter another call." He wrote the order.

"She'll probably have me committed this time." Jain muttered.

Everyone laughed.

"What's going on?" The doctor wanted to know.

A couple of nurses told him the story of Mrs. Hunter's visit to Roni, and how she treated Jain. He shook his head.

"Still, it must have helped, though. We haven't had her back in here, and I haven't treated her in the office."

Everyone snickered again, and as they started to tell him what they knew about Roni, Jain escaped to the nurse's lounge. She knew that the doctor needed to know, that it was all told in confidence, and that they'd never tell it to outsiders, but she was not going to get involved if she could help it: Not in Ray and Roni's problems. At times like this, she would find herself thinking that maybe they did like it, those women who were taking the beatings, then she remembered her marriage to Ray, how he told her that she was nothing, how he was always putting her down, and how she had felt like she was walking on eggshells to keep him from being upset. She remembered that even a short time ago, he had put a hole in her wall, and she had thought that he was going to hit her. Now, she knew that she would fight back, but there was a time when she wouldn't have. It made her so mad!

The doctor knocked and stuck his head in the lounge. "You okay?"

"Yes."

"I wrote some stat orders."

"Yes sir." Her tone was sharp.

He gave her a quizzical look and left. She went to sign off and process the orders. When Elvia's husband came to visit, Jain stayed busy on the other end of the hall. It was a long day, and when she got home, she couldn't forget about it as she usually did.

That night, she lay in her bed thinking about so many things. She thought about the life that she used to live, and couldn't believe that she had been like that. She thought about how much she had changed and how hard it had been to do it. She missed her innocence and then wondered if she had been innocent or ignorant. The most frightening thought of all was that if Ray hadn't left her, she would still be living like that, caught in a trap, existing only to please others. She'd be teaching her kids to be like that. She would have never even known there was another way of life. Way down deep in her heart, she still longed for the fairy tale, the husband, wife and kids and the happily ever after stuff, but she didn't really believe that it existed anymore. She knew her heart had hardened, and it grieved her. She could feel her life changing daily, and didn't know if it was good or bad. She had to go on, no matter what. She had to be strong for the children.

She no longer cried at the sad words of an old country song. She could feel the hard shell around her, and she could still feel the bitterness knawing away at her insides. The negative feelings and sometimes the hatred that she felt toward Ray and Roni ate at her and drained the strength from her body. Sometimes she felt as if she had lost herself and a stranger had taken her place.

In the middle of all this, she thought, 'It's not over. Something else is still coming at me. Why can't it just be over?' She didn't know what she could do. Sometimes, there was no way to help, especially if people didn't seem to want help. About midnight, she fell into a fitful sleep. She dreamed again. She dreamed that she and the children had their house built, that the yard was neat and clean, but the house was in an alcove, and a man in a garbage truck had backed up to the house and was dumping garbage on her house.

The next morning, she overslept. She barely got the kids to school on time, then went back home for coffee and a little more rest before she did her shopping. Jill was restless, so Jain let her out in the back yard. Unable to rest, she decided to go ahead and get the shopping done. She scanned the parking lot of the biggest grocery store in town and when she saw no signs of Ray or Roni, she parked her car and went inside. She really hoped that she wouldn't see anyone that she knew. She felt like hibernating. Her bad mood seemed to be getting worse. She walked down the isle, filling her cart, lost in the thoughts of her own little world, head hung down and a frown on her brow.

Someone bumped her lightly from behind with a buggy.

"Jain!"

She turned around and managed a smile for Lisa. "Hi, looks like we had the same idea. It's easier to get this done while the kids are in school."

"Sure is, I've even got help today." Lisa smiled as a man came around the corner of the other isle. "This is my husband, Jim."

Jain looked up and started to speak. Suddenly all the blood drained from her face and she couldn't say a word. It was the man that she'd seen with Roni at the hamburger joint. Jim was equally shocked. Lisa grabbed Jain's arm, giving him a moment to recover.

"What is it? Jain, what's wrong? You're as white as a sheet!"

Jain thought quickly, then grabbed her stomach. "Must have been something I ate. It's been a rough week. I just had a cramp. I'm feeling better now."

"It sure has. It feels good to have a few days off. Well, we'd better get this shopping done. Hope you feel better."

Jain paid for what was in her cart and went home.

She paced the floor, thinking about Lisa. What should she do? Lisa was her friend. She couldn't tell her what she knew! It would destroy her. Still, she had a right to know. Jim was Lisa's life. She probably wouldn't believe it if someone did tell her. "Oh my God!" Jain realized that her friends must have felt the same way when this was happening to her. For the first time, she understood. She felt a small lump of resentfulness leave her soul, leaving in its place a feeling of weakness and helplessness. Poor Lisa!

Maybe Jim would come to his senses. After all, some people worked out their marital problems. And Ray! If he loved anyone, he loved Roni. Did he know what Roni was doing? If so, was that why he beat her? Was he even the one doing the beating? Jain wasn't sure of anything anymore, especially how or why she was involved in it. She wanted no part of it, yet she could feel the danger all around her. It messed up her life and affected her children. That's what she resented the most. She felt that Roni was only after Jim because she knew that Lisa was a friend. Why? Ray was no longer a part of her life, at least he wouldn't be, if they didn't want to cause trouble. Why did they hold such a grudge? Roni seemed to live just to torment Jain, at least that's how it felt.

Jain put the groceries away, cleaned the house, and then called Lucy. She needed to talk. The phone rang and rang. Lucy wasn't home. Unable to shake the restlessness, she loaded Jill in the car and went to see Brenda. She had to talk to someone. After she'd told her sister everything she knew and everything that she was feeling, she said: "I just don't understand. What is Roni trying to do? Why does she want to ruin people's lives? Bren, I know you think that I'm crazy, but I just know that something awful is going to happen. I don't know what to do about it."

"Jain!" Brenda was exasperated. "I've already told you that you can't do anything about it. Roni is a little tramp who loves trouble. You can't fix the whole world. I don't know why you keep trying. Yes, Lisa will probably get hurt and she doesn't deserve it, but she will get over it. As for Ray, he deserves what he gets."

Jill whimpered in agreement. Jain changed the subject and tried to put it all out of her mind. She got home about fifteen minutes before the kids got home from school. The children were the best comfort in the world for Jain. As she listened to them talk about things that they wanted to do and places that they wanted to go, she calmed down. Cass wanted to see a real, live bear and Stan wanted to see some Indians. Jain knew what he meant. He wanted to see the ceremonies, the dances, and the costumes. He had wanted this since he had discovered that his great, great grandma was one-half Cherokee. This is something that I can do, Jain thought. Secretly she made plans to take the kids to the Great Smoky Mountains in Pigeon Ford when school was out. It would be a surprise.

Chapter 7

When Jain went to work the next day, she learned that they had to work short handed. She sighed and resigned herself to the fact that it would be a busy night. She was surprised to find that Lisa was the nurse who had called in. It wasn't like her to do that. She usually tried to get overtime. She always needed more money.

"What's wrong with Lisa?"

"No one knows. This is the second day in a row that she has called in. That new director of nursing is really mad. She said that Lisa had better be here tomorrow, or she'd be looking for a job."

Jain had to cover the ER and pass meds. on the floor. She didn't stop until eight-thirty, when things finally slowed down and she took her supper break.

She hurriedly ate her sandwich and drank a coke, and then she called Lisa. When Lisa answered, Jain could tell that she'd been crying. This also was unlike Lisa. Jain felt the familiar fear, and that strange feeling that something was very wrong, seep through her body.

"Lisa, are you alright? We've been worried about you. I wanted to warn you that the new D.O.N. is upset."

Lisa started to cry again. Jain could hear the heart retching sobs over the phone.

"Lisa, talk to me. Tell me what's wrong. I'll help you if I can."

"There's nothing that you can do." The broken words were uttered between sobs.

"There might be. Try me." At least, Jain thought, I can get her to talk, let some of the hurt out. "You're my friend, Lisa, I care about you."

Lisa blurted it out. “Jim left me!”

Lisa was crying harder, heartwretching sobs, and Jain was shocked speechless. She had feared that this would happen, but at the same time, she didn’t think that Jim was that stupid. Didn’t he know what a treasure he had in Lisa? How could he throw that away for someone like Roni? Jain was shocked silent.

Lisa’s sobs began to subside. “Jain? Are you still there?”

“I’m here Lisa. I’ll be there to see you as soon as I get off work. When did he leave?”

“Day before yesterday. When I got up, he told me he was leaving. I thought he was kidding. I thought it was a joke.” She started to cry again. “I reached out to touch him and he backed away.”

“Where are the kids?”

"Asleep. I feed them and dress them and send them to school. That's all I can do. They just follow me around and look sad. I feel like a zombie."

Jain remembered the feelings so well. She could help Lisa, and she would. Instead of going home, she would go to Lisa's. The kids were at Brenda's anyway, and she was on evening shift again the next day. She could sleep late in the morning. She was sure that Lisa wasn't eating or sleeping.

The ward clerk stuck her head in the door. "Jain, Mr. Jones wants his pain shot."

"I'll be there in a minute."

"He's getting very upset."

"Lisa, I have to go now. I'll be there when I get off. I'll bring food. Hang in there." Jain went back to work. She didn't tell anyone what was wrong with Lisa, and even though they were all curious, they didn't ask outright.

Ten minutes before time to give report and go home, they had a patient come to the ER. Jain and the aide went to take care of them. Jain would get the information, do the eval, and call the Dr. on call. The aide would stay with the patient while Jain gave report and the shift changed, that is if it was a minor problem. That way, they would get out on time. If it were a true emergency, of course, it wouldn't work that way.

The patient turned out to be Roni Davis. Just my luck, thought Jain, tonight of all nights, she would have to show up. She smiled at Roni, and picked up the ER form.

"What's wrong with you tonight?" Jain noticed fresh scratches on Roni's face and arms. This was different. Not a bruise in sight tonight, and Roni seemed to be bubbling over with happiness.

"I want Lisa to be my nurse." Roni ignored the question that Jain had asked.

"Lisa is not working tonight. You'll have a different nurse in a few minutes. The shift is about to change. If it's nothing too serious, you can wait until then if you want to."

"Why isn't Lisa here? She was supposed to work all week."

"You'll have to ask her, now, what's your complaint tonight?"

"You know, I think I'm feeling better. I'm just going to go. Jim's waiting for me outside." She smiled and sashayed to the door. Jain noticed that Roni had gained some weight. "Hey Jain, Ray will be gone longer this trip. He got to Texas yesterday, and the motor blew in his truck. Someone put sugar in his gas tank. Imagine that. He stays broken down on the road more than he stays home these days. Oh well, I'm sure he'll look you up when he gets back."

Jain stood there stunned. Thank God she now had a car with a locked gas cap. Then it hit her, if Ray was in Texas, who put the scratches on Roni? And who in Texas would put sugar in Ray's gas tank? That truck would never have made it to Texas if the sugar had been added while he was in Tennessee.

The aide, Mary, shook Jain's arm. "What's wrong with you? At least now we'll get to go home on time."

Mary was unaware of the danger and the hidden threats that Roni had made, but Jain knew that something was going on and that it wasn't good. If Ray wasn't the one fighting with Roni, was he the one tormenting Jain and the kids? What was going on anyway? Sometimes she doubted her own sanity.

Jain got out of report early and swung by her house. She picked up a sack full of leftovers and Jill and headed for Lisa's. She tied Jill's leash to the porch rail and knocked. Lisa looked awful. Her eyes were red and swollen. She wore no makeup, and hadn't combed her hair. She looked so pale and helpless. She paced the floor and wrung her hands. Jain placed the food on the table and made her sit down.

"What am I going to do?" She spoke more to herself than to Jain.

"Right now, you are going to eat. How long has it been since you ate?"

"Two days ago, I think. Oh God! Has he only been gone two days?"

Jain poured milk into a glass. "Drink this." She placed the glass in Lisa's hands.

Lisa took a swallow. For a moment, Jain thought that she wasn't going to keep it down, but she did. She looked at Jain with desperate eyes. Jain got up and went around and messaged her shoulders. She was so tense. Jain began to tell her about her own experiences. Then she told her that she had to go on. Even if she didn't want to, she had to do it for her children. She said everything that she could think of to give Lisa a reason to go on. An hour later, Lisa was a little more calm. She had managed to drink a glass of milk and eat a sandwich.

Jain searched the cabinets for something to help Lisa sleep. She found a bottle of Librium with Jim's name on it in the bathroom. There were two pills left in the bottle, and she took one to Lisa, who swallowed it like an obedient child, and Jain wanted to cry. Thirty minutes later, Lisa was asleep on the sofa and Jain couldn't leave her, so she drifted into a fitful sleep in the recliner.

She dreamed that a man was trying to kill her. He was stalking her. She couldn't see his face, only the form of him, and he was wearing a hat. The dream was so real that she could feel the fear surrounding her. In the dream, she had called the police, but they were a long way off. She could here the sirens in the distance. They were getting louder and coming closer, but so was the man. She knew that the police weren't going to get there in time. She tried to run, but couldn't move.

Suddenly she jolted awake and realized that the sound she had heard was the alarm clock in Lisa's bedroom. She got up and cut it off. Lisa slept on. When the children got up, Jain fed them, and helped them get dressed, then she let them watch TV in their room. At ten, Jain woke Lisa. They both had to go to work that evening. Lisa needed to stop crying and get mad. Jain knew she had to tell her about Jim and Roni.

"Lisa, wake up. We have to go to work today. We have to find someone to keep your kids."

Lisa was groggy as she rubbed the sleep from her eyes. "Jim——" The words died on her lips. "Jain, I can't go to work. Jim left me."

"You can go to work. You have your children who depend on you. You can make it. There are some things you have to know. Can your Mom keep your kids today and tonight?"

"Will you call her? She doesn't know. I can't talk to her about it now. I need more time. How will I ever get through this?"

Jain called Lisa's mom. She told her only that Jim wasn't home tonight and that Lisa couldn't miss anymore work. She offered to bring the kids over. She had the kids give Lisa a big hug, and then she took them to Lisa's mom, two blocks away. When she returned, she and Lisa sat at the kitchen table with a pot of strong, black coffee. Jain was glad to see that Lisa was doing better with the coffee than she had with the milk the night before. Jain got up and made toast and scrambled eggs. She placed a plate in front of Lisa and was relieved to see Lisa eat every bite. Jain took a deep breath. She had to tell her; she had put it off as long as she could.

"Lisa, I have to tell you something. Jim was with Roni last night. He brought her to the ER. She made a point of telling me - - that and that Ray was broken down in Texas. I hope that you don't get mad at me for telling you. I understand now why no one would tell me about Ray when this was happening to me. The first time that I saw Jim and Roni together, I talked myself out of telling you. I even convinced myself that it wasn't true. Jain swallowed hard. "Someone had to tell you. I wish it didn't have to be me."

Lisa shoved the plate and the coffee cup to the floor with one swipe of her arm.

"That's not true! Why would you say that, Jain? I thought you were my friend!"

"Lisa, I am your friend. You know I am. If I didn't tell you, someone else would. I thought it would be best if you found out here at home instead of at work or some other public place." Jain reached a hand toward Lisa.

"No!" Lisa backed away. "Why would you say something like that? Just because it happened to you doesn't mean that's what happened to me. I don't believe you." Lisa was mad at Jain.

Jain remembered that feeling well. She remembered getting mad at the people who had tried to tell her about Ray. She had thought that they were troublemakers. She sat in her chair and watched as Lisa vented her feelings. She tried not to take the hateful remarks personally. Finally, Lisa slumped back into her chair. She looked at Jain with her broken heart in her eyes.

"Are you sure, Jain? Is it really true? Is this really happening to me?"

"Yes, Lisa. I wish it weren't. I wish I could make it go away. You have to be strong. You have to for the children's sake. What's more, we have to go to work today. That new D.O.N. has said that if you don't work today, you're fired. You really need your job now."

Jain didn't have the heart to tell her that she would have to hire a lawyer, and have a full time baby sitter and pay all the bills besides.

"I can't do it."

"Sure you can. I'll help you. If Roni is there, you keep your distance."

"That would be about like her, wouldn't it? To get herself admitted just to see me suffer. I think she is insane. I've never seen anyone be so mean."

Jain nodded. "Take a shower and get dressed. I'll take Jill home and get ready for work, and then I'll be back and pick you up. If Roni is there, we'll get her a psychological evaluation. Maybe we can even get her committed."

Lisa managed a very weak laugh.

When Jain got home, she wasn't really surprised to find a note stuck on her door, telling her to mind her own business.

It was a rough week. The days dragged by. Lisa finally found her inner strength and was able to do her job. Jain continued to support her friend and was relieved to see that Lisa's family rallied around her. Lisa moved in with her mother for awhile.

Jain made plans for vacation. She needed it and so did the kids. She was exhausted and the kids were cranky. Two more days and they would be headed for the mountains. They were already packed. All they had to do was load the car and take Jill to Brenda's. They were all excited.

Chapter 8

They had the trunk full of suitcases, plenty of easy to care for, comfortable cloths. Cass and Jain were in the front seat, and Stan was in the back seat with the cooler of food and drinks. Jain had gassed up the car the night before. They drove fifty miles out of town, and then headed east on interstate 40, toward Knoxville. It would be a six to eight hour trip to Pigeon Forge. The kids were bouncing on the seats with excitement. Jain smiled. She planned to stop at every single rest stop that she came to.

In between the rest stops, the children made big plans, or played games. Jain listened to the monotonous tones of "I spy, with my little eye —-," and tried not to let it get on her nerves. It was great to see them so happy and excited. She soon forgot about work, Lisa's problems, and even her own. She even joined in the children's games. About four in the afternoon, they pulled off I-40 onto the road that would take them into Pigeon Forge and up to the cabin that they had rented for the next five days. The children's faces were glued to the windows as they looked at all the attractions and billboards of the things they wanted to do.

The rustic-looking cabin was nestled into the trees on a steep mountain road. It was almost hidden. Jain had to look closely to find the driveway. There was a steep drop off into a hollow behind it. All you could see were trees. On the side was a steep hillside, also covered with trees. Even though there were other cabins less than half a mile away, there was a marvelous feeling of isolation. It was like she and her children were alone in the world, with only a car passing occasionally and a distant voice drifting on the wind once in a while. There was a narrow porch on the side and back of the cabin, with a grill and around back was a hot tub. It seemed like heaven.

Jain sat in the rocker and breathed deeply of the clean mountain air, while the kids raced about exploring their new surroundings. The cabin was one story, but there was stairs leading up to a loft that served as a bedroom. Stan laid claim to that. The other bedroom was in back, and that's where Cass stashed her things. The sofa in the living room made a bed and that's where Jain would sleep. Soon the car was unloaded and the kids had discovered that the television worked. Jain was tired, but their energy was boundless.

"Momma, where are we going to eat?"

"Yeah, I'm hungry!"

Jain popped her feet upon the rail of the porch. "Let's finish up all that food that we brought with us tonight. In the morning, we will go down to the pancake house and have blueberry pancakes. Then you two can ride that roller coaster and that giant water slide. We'll check out all those little amusement parks and rides tomorrow. That long trip has made me tired."

Evidently, Jain wasn't the only one that was tired. After they ate and cleaned up the mess, they all sat on the sofa bed to watch television. It was already getting dark, but they didn't bother to turn on the lights. Engrossed in the movie, Jain was surprised to hear someone snore. She looked around and saw that both her children were sound asleep. When the movie ended, she cut the television off with the remote control, and soon drifted off to sleep, lying across the bed at her children's feet.

She was dreaming again, but it wasn't a nightmare. Someone was rattling the door. She gradually roused from a deep, restful sleep. Oh no, she thought, for there really was a noise outside. She crept to the window and looked out. Ten feet away, was a big black bear rummaging around the garbage can. She had forgotten to bring it inside. Quietly, she went back to the bed and gently woke Cass.

"What is it?"

"SH—-," She motioned Cass to the window and pointed out the bear that could be seen very well in the moonlit night.

"Oh!" breathed Cass. Her eyes were huge as she stared at the bear. Her mouth was still held in the shape of an o, and her hands were on the windowpanes.

Jain had stopped watching the bear, and was watching her daughter. She had thought that the only bears that Cass would see, would be the ones in cages that you paid admission to see. This moment that she shared with her daughter made the whole trip worthwhile. Eventually, the bear loped off, and they went back to bed. Jain drifted off to sleep still planning ways to make this vacation memorable for her children.

The next morning, the sun shining through the window on her face awakened Jain. She stretched and yawned. She awoke the kids, then took a quick shower. She desperately wanted a cup of coffee. The children were hungry. They drove to a parking lot near the pancake house and parked. When they couldn't eat another bite, they walked down the sidewalk, taking in every site. They stopped at the water slide, and the children rode down that several times. They went on to the roller coaster, then to the bumper cars.

They played a round of miniature golf. When they got tired of walking, they rode the trolley cars. They checked out all the attractions on both sides of the street.

When Jain heard the familiar cries of "Mom, I'm hungry," she looked at her watch. It was nearly five p.m. They found a place to eat, then took the trolley back to the car. Back at the cabin, the kids tried out the hot tub. They were sound asleep by eight. Jain counted her money. She had spent more than planned that first day, but the kids had really enjoyed the day. She made plans for the next day. She would take them to the campgrounds in the park and let them do the free stuff. They would hike and cook out. She checked out the kitchen and the supplies, then threw a couple of iron skillets and charcoal into a box. The first stop in the morning would be a grocery store. This time, Jain had the sofa bed all to herself. She stretched and yawned, then fell asleep, feeling relaxed and safe. This night, she didn't dream. Before she knew it, Stan was shaking her.

"Get up Mom! You are wasting our vacation."

She groaned, turned over and closed her eyes. Words failed her. It was a wonderful vacation. What was that kid talking about? But she knew. He was anxious to be doing something. Cass was also up and ready to go. Jain had no choice. She rolled out of bed, took a quick shower, and dressed in blue jeans and a tee shirt.

"Ok kids, grab that box and get in the car. Off we go."

"Where are we going today Momma? What are we going to do?"

"First we are going to the grocery store. Then we are going to cook bacon and eggs and coffee over an open fire. Are you hungry?"

"Yes." Both children answered at once.

After breakfast, they hiked along the mountain trails, taking in all the beauty of the majestic mountains. They stopped at a designated spot and looked out over the Great Smoky Mountains, at the clouds rising up, which looked like smoke in the distance.

"That's how the mountains got their name." Jain explained to the children. "Isn't it beautiful up here?"

"I wish we could stay here always." Cass said this softy.

"Me too." Echoed Stan.

Jain remained quiet. She too wished that it could be like this forever, but she knew that it would end soon.

They climbed to the top of Klingmans' Dome and their legs were tired and their muscles ached. Jain snapped pictures of the kids. They went back to the park and cooked hamburgers for a late lunch then the kids played in the babbling, white waters of the little brook that was near-by. The water was made white by flowing so fast against the rocks as it raced down the mountain. It was beautiful. Jain snapped more pictures of the children, this time as they played in the stream.

At the end of the day, they were exhausted, and fell into bed as soon as they got back to the cabin. The next morning, everyone slept until ten. It was eleven by the time they ate breakfast. Jain decided to drive over the mountain into North Carolina and let Stan see an Indian. She knew that they did dances and that you could even have a picture made with an Indian in full dress, feathers and all. She'd let Stan get his picture made. She wished that she could afford to take the children to see the drama "Trail of Tears" but she knew that she couldn't. She bought each child a pair of moccasins and an indian blanked. Once again, she spent more than she had planned to spend. It would be the pleasures of nature again the next day, but that was ok. It was Jain's favorite part of the trip, and the kids also enjoyed it. When the last day of their vacation rolled around, they hit the outlet malls. She bought the children a few name brand cloths. She let them go on the water slide once more, and then they went back to the cabin and packed.

It had been a good vacation. No one wanted it to end. She reminded the kids that Jill was waiting, and they headed for home.

The trip home was different. They made less rest stops. It was filled with questions like: "Are we there yet?" "How much longer 'till we are there?" "Can we get Jill tonight?" Jain made the trip home in six hours, but it seemed to take forever. About five miles from home, they came upon a giant red and white striped tent, filled with metal folding chairs. A couple of men were setting up microphones. A few cars were already parked in the field next to the tent.

"What's that?" asked Stan.

"Is it a circus?" Cass wanted to know.

"No, it's a tent revival." Jain told them. "The sign says it will be here for a week."

"What's a tent revival?" Stan wanted to know.

"It's kind of like church, only you have it outside under a tent. They have singing and preaching. The sign says this preacher is an evangelist."

"Can we go?" This came from Cass.

Well, why not, thought Jain. What kind of mother would tell her child that she couldn't go to church? The tent may fall on me, but if she wants to go, I'm going to take her. She pulled into a parking place. By now, others were arriving. As they made their way into the tent to find seats, people came to greet them with hugs and handshakes, making them feel welcome.

"This is like that church where Momma used to go." Cass whispered this in Stan's ear, but Jain heard it.

Yeah, it is, Jain thought, but she didn't say anything. She felt peculiar, as she sat beside her children and waited for the service to begin. She really missed that part of the life that she used to have. She sometimes felt so empty now.

The atmosphere came alive when they started singing the old time gospel songs. Folks were standing and clapping their hands in time to the music. The piano and guitars seemed to have a life of their own. The tent seemed to vibrate. You could feel the power in the air. Jain knew what it was, but she had been away from it for so long that she was surprised that she could still recognize the Spirit of God. The empty spot inside her seemed ten times bigger than usual, and she knew she was going to cry. The tears slid silently down her cheeks and the preaching hadn't even started. The children stood at her side watching, not saying a word. Their eyes were wide and they leaned closer to their mother. Jain knew that they were frightened, but she was dealing with her own emotions.

She was vaguely aware when the fear left them and they joined in, clapping their hands in time to the music, but she was still consumed by her own emotions. Most folks were standing, but she remained seated. Her wobbly legs wouldn't hold her up.

Sitting there, feeling the Spirit all around her, Jain gripped the seat of her chair on either side. Her knuckles were white. She hardly breathed. She had a death hold on that chair, and she wasn't even aware of it. Already, she could feel the gentle, drawing of the Spirit and the preaching hadn't even started. It was like there was an invisible line that was connected to the altar on one end and to her heart on the other, and someone was gently tugging it, drawing her toward the alter. She resisted. It was all she could do to sit there. She thought about getting up and going outside. She thought about going to the altar. She sat there squirming in her seat. The gentle tug became stronger.

She didn't really hear the preachers' words, as he talked about the forgiveness of sins and God's love, but she knew the story well. It had been written in her heart many years ago. When the service ended and the preacher gave the altar call they started singing "Softly and tenderly Jesus is calling." Jain stood up. She was still holding the chair. She took a determined step toward the altar. She dropped the chair somewhere in the isle, and continued on without missing a step.

The next thing she knew was that she was on her knees at the altar, and all she could say was "Jesus," but that was enough. As the tears poured from her eyes and the words poured from her mouth, she felt Him come back into her heart. She felt the peace that had so long eluded her return. She felt the fear and hatred leave her body. She felt clean again for the first time in years. She was made whole again. Jain rejoiced in the spirit. She felt as light as a feather. She left that revival knowing that she was not alone. She and the children had help. She would not forget it again. She knew her trials were not over, but she knew that she would make it. It was the first time that she'd felt real peace since her divorce. She glowed with happiness.

It was almost midnight by the time they picked up Jill. Brenda was still up. All the lights were on. Jain had expected her to be asleep.

"Jain! I was so worried!"

"I'm sorry, Bren. There was a tent revival and we stopped there. Bren, I went back to the altar! I feel so good!" She hugged her sister.

"No, Jain, you don't understand! There was a wreck. A car just like yours went off that big hill between here and town. It happened just a few hours ago. A big truck ran it off the road. They haven't released the names of the victims, but it was a woman and two kids. I went out there, but the scene is still blocked off. Some kids were parked off that little dirt road at the top of the hill. They heard a gun shot and saw the wreck. They told the police that they heard a shot, then saw the truck ram the car from behind. There was a man and a woman in the truck, but they couldn't identify them. The man was driving. They didn't know who was in the car. We heard about it when we went to the gas station. We went to the police station, but they wouldn't tell us anything. I've been going out of my mind, we thought that it was you. You'd better call Mom!" Brenda stopped to catch her breath. She was still as pale as a ghost, and her eyes were red from crying.

Jain made the call, even though she had to wake her mom. She also called the hospital. Lisa was also glad to hear from Jain. She had a little more information. Bill had been out to get a cup of coffee, and had filled her in.

"You should have seen him, Jain. He was so shaken up. I think he thought it was you and the kids. He was white as a sheet. I felt sorry for him. The woman died. The ambulance brought her out to be pronounced, but the kids were ok. It was the gun shot that killed her, not the wreck."

Jain knew that she should be afraid, but somehow, she wasn't. She only felt sadness that someone had lost their life and especially that those children had lost their mother. She told Lisa that she would see her tomorrow, and held her own kids a little tighter. Despite all this, Jain slept like a baby.

Chapter 9

Everyone noticed the change in Jain. At work the next day, they said; “You must have a new boyfriend.” Or; “You sure look rested.” Or; “Did you color your hair?” Some would come right out and say, “What happened to you? You’re like a different person.”

Jain tried to tell them, but they really didn’t want to hear about her religious experience. Some of her Christian friends from her past did make a point to come around and offer support. Jain was grateful. She started going to church on the Sundays that she didn’t have to work. The first time was awkward, for her and for everyone else.

Lisa noticed the difference in Jain more than anyone else did. They were still friends, but there was now a distance between them, a strain that wasn’t there before. Jain could feel it and she reached out to her friend. She knew what Lisa was going through. She wanted to be there for her. She invited Lisa to go to church with her, but Lisa wouldn't. Jain remembered the feeling. When Lisa went out to a bar, Jain wouldn't go with her. She'd never been much of a party person, and neither had Lisa. Now, they were both having major life changes. Lisa went to places that she had never been before. Jain didn't want to loose her friend. Lisa put on a good act, but Jain knew that she wasn't happy. It really was an act.

Most folks thought that Lisa was happier than ever. On the surface, she was more bubbly and outgoing. She wore more make-up. She had lost weight and dressed better. She had a quick smile that didn't quite reach her eyes, but most folks didn't look that deep. Jain could feel Lisa's pain. It was stronger than the empathy that nurses normally had. She felt so helpless and didn't know how to help her friend. There was an invisible wall between them.

Jim wasn't happy either and it showed. He also, had lost weight. His eyes had a hollow look. He could still be found with Roni when Ray was out of town, but he looked like a little lost puppy following her around. When it was his weekend to have the kids, Roni was not with them. For that matter, she was hardly ever seen with her own child.

Jain wished that Roni couldn't cause so much trouble. She knew that Roni still had some kind of hold on Jim. She could see the misery that she had caused for Lisa and Jim. She had not forgotten what part Roni had played in ending her marriage to Ray and the misery that it had caused for her children. She knew that if Ray loved anyone, he loved Roni. For some time now, Jain had thought that Roni really was crazy. Now she wondered if Roni was demon possessed. No mere mortal could like trouble that much. She had to sit up nights to figure out her evil schemes. Jain almost felt sorry for her. She now thought that Roni had done her a favor by taking Ray. She truly knew that her life was better without him, and she also knew that she would have never left him. This made it easier to take care of Roni when she was in the hospital.

This time, Roni came in with nausea, abdominal pain, and amenorea. Jain and Lisa found this out during report when they went to work. Her diagnosis was dehydration, possibly due to pregnancy. Dana informed them that Roni was now tolerating food and fluids well. Lab had been done, but they were still waiting on the results. The machine was broken, and they wouldn't have results until the next day because they had to send all the labs out. Dana was feeling sorry for Roni. She said that it would be hard on Roni, having another baby with her husband away so much.

"I might be pregnant." Roni smiled at Jain and Lisa as they passed her room. She stood just inside the door. "Of course if it's Jim's, he will have to do like Ray and not pay child support." She looked at Lisa and smiled broader.

Lisa took a deep breath in and stood up taller. Her fists clenched. She took a step toward Roni who stood propped up against the wall, still smiling. Jain grabbed her friend by the arm that she had started to raise and turned her away from the door. She knew that if Lisa hit a patient, she would loose her job. With new insight, she was aware that Roni also knew that. Roni was trying to get Lisa in trouble. As she forcefully walked her friend away from the room, she saw the light above the door come on. Roni had hit the nurse call light.

"Jain, will one of you get that?" called the ward clerk.

"No!" Jain lowered her voice. "Page Mary to see what she wants."

"But you are standing right there. Mary is down at the end of the hall."

"Page Mary or let her wait." Jain, with a tight grip on Lisa's arm marched her to the nurses' lounge. The next day, Lisa would have a bruise from Jain's tight grip and her resistance. Once they were inside, Jain closed the door and let her go. The lounge was empty and Jain leaned against the door.

Lisa viscously kicked the sofa into the wall, then pounded on the back of it with both fists. Jain kept her distance and kept quiet until some of the rage had passed.

Lisa sat on the sofa, pale as a ghost; all the blood had drained from her face. “I’m going to kill her.” She spoke quietly now. “I’ll smother her with her pillow the next time I go into her room. I’m sure she will want it plumped as soon as she sees me in the hall, and I know she’ll want me to do it for her. She’s not going to rob my children of what little they have left of their dad.”

Jain reached a hand toward her friend. “Lisa - - -,”

“Don’t preach to me Jain. Don’t tell me to let it go or to forgive her. I’ll forgive her when hell freezes over. Have you seen Jim? Have you seen what she’s done to him? He hardly looks human anymore. The world would be better off without her in it. Religion or not, you have to admit that. Now I know what you went through, what you still go through. I'm glad that you got over Ray, but I'm not over Jim! I never will be. I'm not as strong as you are. I hate him and I love him. I can't believe that I ever felt sorry for that witch, Roni! It makes me sick to think that I was nice to her. How could I have felt sorry for her?"

Lisa dissolved into tears. Jain made an unethical decision. She went to the nurse's station and called the doctor. When he came on the line, she said: "You know that Roni Davis, in room ten? She is tolerating her food and fluids well. She says she may be pregnant. She has had no bleeding and no further pain. Can we discharge her now?"

She knew that the doctor probably thought that Roni wanted to go home, and she felt guilty for deceiving him. She would get on her knees and beg

God's forgiveness tonight. She would also pray for Lisa and Jim.

"I suppose so. I was going to do more tests tomorrow, but if she wants to go, go ahead and discharge her. We can do them in the office."

Jain got the papers ready. She had the ward clerk to call Ray to come get Roni, and then she went and packed her things. Roni had just started to rage and throw a fit when Ray walked into the room.

"Great news, Baby. I didn't think they'd let you go tonight. We'll have more time together now. I really hate it when I have to leave you, especially the long hauls like Texas." He put his arms around her.

Roni's fit ceased immediately. She wrapped her arms around Ray's neck and glared at Jain over his shoulder. Jain knew she would pay later, still she smiled at Roni.

"Have a nice night. You're ready to go."

Lisa came out of the lounge as Ray and Roni reached the end of the hall. Her color was a little better. Jain smiled but Lisa didn't.

"I know what you did, Jain!"

Jain poked her friend in the ribs. "I know who you are and I saw what you did." Jain mimicked the line from the movie. Lisa didn't think it was funny.

They had a patient comming through the emergency room. The ambulance message was fading in and out over the scanner. "- - - hospital- - male with chest pain - - - Oh s- - - - Starting CPR. ETA one to two minutes. Over."

The ward clerk acknowledged the message and called the doctor. He would be on his way. Jain and Lisa ran to the ER. They got the IV, O2, and monitor ready. They checked the life-pack and unlocked the crash cart. They knew one person would be driving and one doing CPR. They had both done their share of ambulance runs. They didn't have paramedics; only E M T's, but Jain and Lisa knew that they were good at their job and that they would help them work the code. As the ambulance backed in, Lisa held the door open, and Jain helped unload the patient. He was in the ER almost by the time the driver of the ambulance cut the motor. Lisa was now doing compressions and Adam was bagging the patient. Steve, the driver, grabbed the laryngoscope and ET tube from the crash cart.

"Hyperventilate him."

He inserted the ET tube as Jain slid the eighteen-gauge angiocath into the vein of his left arm. She collected blood prior to running the fluids, for she knew that by now, lab was on the way. She was surprised that the doctor wasn't there already. Xray would also come in. A hospital this small couldn't keep all departments present on all shifts, but they all took call and responded well.

"Bilateral breath sounds," The ambu bag was now attached to O2.

Adam checked for a pulse, then took over compressions.

Lisa attached the monitor. "Asystole"

Jain charged the paddles to 200j. "Stand clear!" She shocked the patient and looked at the monitor. Still a flat line. She pushed epinephrine 1.0mg and watched the monitor. Nothing. She charged the paddles to 300j. She called the all clear and shocked him again. When he still didn't convert, she pushed the lidocaine bolus. She upped the fluids, and Lisa inserted a Foley catheter. All this took place as CPR continued. Jain repeated the epinephrine. Adam and Steve had traded places. Chest compressions were hard work. Jain charged the paddles to 360j, called the clear and defibrillated one more time. Nothing. She repeated the lidocaine and saw the pattern start on the monitor. She hung a lidocaine drip. They stopped compressions. The doctor arrived and Lisa gave him a report. Random BP checks had been 0, but now was 90/50.

"Does he have urine output?" The doctor was listening to the patient's chest.

"30 cc, very dark."

"Put him on the respirator. Get a chest Xray, lytes, cbc, blood gasses- - -," Lab took the samples from Jain's hand. The doctor was interrupted as the patient's family rushed in. If the machines were still down, they would unlock the doctor's office next door and run the tests there. Family rushed into the emergency room.

"We want him sent to Nashville!" These were the first words out of their mouths.

"It's not a good idea to move him. He's not stable. His heart stopped and he's still not breathing on his own. We are getting ready to put him on the respirator and put him in the special care room. A nurse will stay with him at all times."

"No. We want him in Nashville where they can do more for him. He needs a specialist" This came from a big blond girl with a curly perm. Jain figured that she was the patient's daughter.

"Look, if you move him now, he could die." The doctor almost pleaded with them, but it did no good. The medical team feared that their efforts were for nothing.

They made arrangements for the medical helicopter to come and get the patient. The doctor did manage to talk them into letting him put the man on the respirator and have a nurse stay with him until the chopper arrived. They put him in room ten. It was near the nurses' station. He was there for about two hours before he was transported.

Jain and Lisa sat at the desk working on his chart and discharge paperwork.

"Too bad we couldn't keep him," said the ward clerk. "Especially since we sent Roni home. At least she wanted to stay with us." She looked at Jain when she said this. It was easy to see she was still mad.

Jain and Lisa looked at each other and burst out laughing. It was a release of tension as much as anything else, but Sandy, the ward clerk didn't know that.

"I don't see what's so funny! It won't be either one of you that has to stay home because the census is low!

Especially not Miss Goody Two Shoes Jain! She's the RN!" She stomped off down the hall. They saw her stop and talk to Mary. Heads bobbed up and down as they talked. They took turns glancing toward the nursing station.

As their peels of laughter died away, Lisa stood and put her hand on Jain's shoulder. They both knew that they had reconnected. Their friendship was no longer strained. It was alive and strong. "Thank you, Miss Goody Two Shoes. Thank you for bringing me food and for keeping me from loosing my job. And thank you, I guess, for not letting me smother Roni."

"Don't be silly, you would have done the same for me. We're friends."

"I don't know Jain, I'm not as strong as you. I'd take Jim back in a heartbeat."

"I did take Ray back, but it didn't work. If he loves anyone in this world, it's Roni. If he's ever been hurt over anyone, it's her. I don't know what kind of hold she has over them. You know that she has even made us feel sorry for her with those huge tears, a few times anyway. You're so kind-hearted Lisa. You cared more than I did."

"She'll get us for this Jain, especially you. She's worse on you than she is on me. All she does to me is to flaunt her relationship with Jim in my face. I think she would hire a hit man for you if she could. At least she stays away from my home; of course that may be because I put my new mobil home in my parent's yard. I never thought I'd do that. It works out great for the boys, though. They have a revolving door. They go back and forth as they please between Mom's house and mine. Being around my dad keeps them from missing Jim so much. They seem to be ok."

Jain wished her dad hadn't died so young. When he was alive, Ray would not have done all this. He would have been afraid to. Jain shook her head.

"Sometimes I think she has hired a hit man. Really strange men drive by my house sometimes. People have tried to break in. I try to tell myself that it's just Ray and that he just wants to frighten me, but I'm not sure. God will protect us though. Looking back, I can see that he helped me even when I wasn't trying to live right."

"Now don't preach to me Jain. I'm not ready for that yet. It's time to make rounds. You have to get ready for report."

"You sound like my kids, but you know what's strange is that I don't want Ray back anymore. Why does she still want to torture me?"

Jain picked up the kids and went home. They were so sleepy, barely waking enough to walk to the car and get in. they went back to sleep in the back seat. Jain was grateful for that when she pulled into her driveway. Someone had taken some kind of florescent goo and written dirty words on her door. They glared at her in the headlights of her car. She cut the motor, but left the lights on, then she took the keys, holding one key between her index and middle fingers, incase she needed a weapon to gouge eyes, and locked the kids in the car. She searched the yard, but found nobody. She tried the door. It was still locked. She could here Jill barking inside. Jain opened the door and let her out to guard the car. She went inside and searched the house, even looking in all the closets and under the beds.

When she was satisfied that her home was safe, she brought the kids in and put them to bed, then she tried to calm the agitated dog. "I sure wish you could talk." She stroked the dog's head. She tried again to tell herself that Ray and Roni just wanted to frighten her. The kids slept and the dog calmed down, but Jain couldn't. She got down on her knees and prayed, then she got up and washed the stuff off her door. Thank God, that it came off with hot soapy water and bleach. Still unable to sleep, she sat on the sofa and read her Bible. When she let it fall open, it was at Psalms chapt. 143 and her eyes fell on verses 11 and 12. She read;

> *"11 Quicken me, O Lord, for thy name's sake: for thy righteousness' sake bring my soul out of trouble.*

> *12 And of thy mercy cut off my enemies, and destroy all them that afflict my soul: for I am thy servant."*

Jain looked up. "Lord," she said softly, "I think I need you to do that for me. I know that I'm not supposed to fear. I know that you are always with me, but I am afraid, for the children and for me. I know that vengeance belongs to you. I don't hate them anymore, I really don't, but I sure wish the trouble would stop." Fear left her and she fell asleep on the sofa, her Bible still open on her abdomen.

She awoke to the sound of cartoons on television and when she opened her eyes all the way, she saw Stan and Cass sitting cross-legged on the floor, eating bowls of cereal and laughing at the cartoons. Jill had a big bowl of cereal also and she looked up at Jain and wagged her stub of a tail.

"I'm sorry, Momma, did we wake you? We tried to keep it down."

"Oh No! What time is it?" Jain put her feet on the floor.

"Ten" The kids looked at her funny. "What's wrong?"

She was halfway to the kitchen before she remembered that it was Saturday and she had this week end off. "I guess I just need my coffee," she said over her shoulder. She was glad that she had taken the time to clean up that mess last night. Now the children didn't have to know about it. She heard giggles and peaked around the door. Jill's empty cereal bowl was now a lopsided hat and she sat between the kids, watching television. Jain poured her coffee and joined them.

Steps on the porch startled her, and then she realized that it was only the mailman. She went to get the mail and her heart sank as she pulled out the pink envelope with her name in the familiar childish scrawl. Roni's note went on and on about how Jain was messing up her life and warned her to stop. Jain tossed it in the trash. It wasn't really a surprise. She had known that Roni would make her pay for sending her home from the hospital, but she didn't think it would be this soon. She had to have planned this prior to last night. Jain suspected that there was still more to come. She wasn't going to sit there and wait for it. She wasn't going to waste her day off.

She gathered the kids, dog, and food into the car and they headed down the Natchez Trace Parkway. They went nearly to the Alabama state line, then headed back, stopping at all the historic sites. They spent hours at Metal Ford, where the children and the dog roamed the trails and waded in the shallow part of the river, where the travelers used to "ford" or cross the river on their trips. They pushed the button on the old metal box to hear the history, but never stayed to hear it all. Jain sat on the bank and dangled her feet in the water. It had a soothing effect. She watched the river flow gently in the deepest part, and ripple over the shallow rock bed that was the ford. Beautiful trees grew on both sides of the banks. The water looked green. It was so peaceful that she dreaded to leave. She pulled her feet out of the water and noticed that they were white and the skin was shriveled. She could loose all sense of time, just sitting here and watching the water flow. She thought, 'What a beautiful world God has made.'

“Can we go now? My legs are tired.” The words came from Stan, as he, Cass and Jill plopped down at Jain’s side.

“Yeah, I guess we’d better.” Jain started to get up and realized that she had sat there until she was stiff. The children helped her.

“Momma’s getting old.” This remark came from Cass.

“Old Momma! Old Momma!” Stan chanted as he and Jill ran ahead to the car.

Jain smiled. It was funny, but she actually felt younger these days. Her load felt lighter. The circumstances hadn’t changed, but she knew that she had. When they got home, the kids had a sandwich and a glass of milk, and then Cass hit the shower. Stan fell asleep in front of the TV before she came out of the bathroom. Jain half carried and half walked him to bed.

They are going to be grown before I know it, she thought. A sense of sadness washed over her. What would her life be without her children? Once again she thanked God for them, and she wondered what was wrong with Ray that he couldn't love them. She really felt sorry for him. He didn't know what he had missed.

"Night Mom." Cass sounded half-asleep.

Jain went and kissed her daughter good night, then she and Jill settled on the couch to watch TV. The ring of the phone sounded loud in the quiet of the house. Jain dreaded to answer it. "Hello?"

"How many times do I have to tell you to stop upsetting Roni? If you don't leave her alone, You're going to pay big time! I've warned you before!"

"Ray, I have not done anything to Roni. Try to understand. She has nothing that I want. I want you and Roni to be happy and leave me alone."

"Don't give me that, Jain. Every single time that she sees you, she's upset for days! She told me about you writing her letters. I know that she did that to you when we were married, but it won't work on us. I love her! She is my life. You are nothing. Stay out of our lives."

"Believe me, Ray, I want nothing to do with you or Roni. I just want to live my life in peace. We don't bother you. You don't even have to pay child support. I ask nothing of you, and I don't want you back. What more do you want?"

"Just don't upset Roni and don't start on that child support stuff- - - -,"

Jain hung up on him. When the phone rang again, not two minutes later, she thought it was him calling back. She almost didn't answer it. After seven rings, she picked up the receiver.

"Now look-," She was interrupted.

"Hello Jain. You know, you shouldn't get so uptight. It's not healthy." It was a deep, masculine voice that she had never heard before and it sent frightening chills down her spine.

"Who is this?"

"You looked pretty relaxed at the river. You had a dreamy look on your face. It's kind of quiet at your place tonight. Is that mean-eyed dog of yours asleep?"

"Who is this? I'm calling the police!" She heard the deep-throated laughter before she hung up the phone. She could feel the danger. She sat there trembling for a few minutes, and then she got down on her knees and prayed desperately for protection for her children and for herself. She prayed for hours and finally, she was calm enough to sleep.

The next morning, she and the kids got up and went to church. Jain soaked in every word that the preacher spoke. He talked about how everyone had sinned; still God loved them all. He told them that Jesus himself said that all that ever came before him were thieves and robbers. She felt so unworthy and inadequate. She was hungry for God. She needed him more than she ever had in her life. She listened as the preacher explained that by ourselves, we are nothing, but with God, we are something. He read Philippians chapter four and verse thirteen: *"I can do all things through Christ which stregntheneth me."* The words were burned into Jain's heart. She knew without a doubt that it was true. She remembered how mad she had been when Ray had called her a nothing and a nobody. Wouldn't he be surprised, she thought, to know that he was right. Without God, that's exactly what I am, a nothing and a nobody, but she knew for certain that she would never be without Him again. It was a good weekend after all. She still had a feeling that something bad was going to happen, but she knew that she and the kids would be all right. She would trust in God for their safety.

When the service ended, she ushered the kids out to the car. They shook hands with a few people on the way out, but didn't stay to socialize. Jain felt someone starring at her from across the room and turned to see who it was. Brad stood there starring at her with his arm across the shoulder of a very pretty woman. The woman looked at Brad, then let her eyes travel to Jain, and smiled. Jain managed to smile back, then hurried the kids to the car.

They picked up Jill and went for hamburgers before they settled in for a quiet evening at home. They went by their land where their new home was slowly, but surely being built. It wouldn't be long before they had a home that was really theirs.

About three thirty, Jain heard a car pull into the drive, then footsteps on the porch. Jill growled. That couldn't be good, because Jill usually barked and wagged her stub of a tail when company came by. Jain looked out the window to see Ray standing at the door.

Ray raised his fist to knock as Jain opened the door and Jill barred her teeth. It was a comical sight and Jain heard the children laugh. She took hold of the dog's collar and told Ray to come in. She put the dog in the bedroom, and returned to see the kids trying to talk to Ray. He only grunted at what they said, or else he just ignored them. It broke Jain's heart to see them reaching out to him like that.

"Jain," he spoke as she returned to the room. "I am leaving on a three day haul in the morning. I don't want you upsetting Roni while I'm gone. We still don't know for sure if she's pregnant or not, and I'm warning you not to bother her."

The children went out the back door, and Jain took a deep breath. "Ray, I will be working and the children will be in school all week. We wouldn't have time to bother Roni if we wanted to, and we don't. I'm tired of all the threats and scare tactics. We have our lives and you and Roni have yours. Just let it end. It's over. You don't care about the kids and I don't want you back in my life. You can tell that to Roni."

"You say that, Jain, but I don't believe you. All she has to do is see you and she's upset. Maybe I didn't treat you and the kids right, but I love Roni. She wouldn't hate you so much if you didn't give her a reason to do it. I try so hard to make her happy. I'd do anything for her. Don't you understand?" He was less angry now. He was almost pleading, and Jain felt pity for him.

The trouble was that she did understand. She'd once felt that way about him. Now she was actually feeling sorry for him. "Ray," she said, "You can't make someone love you. I tried that with you. Remember? It doesn't work. You can't change anyone, except for yourself, and that's not easy. I know how hard it is when you loose someone's love."

He was mad again. "Oh shut up Jain! What do you know about anything anyway? Roni is not like you. She does love me. You just leave her alone!"

He got up and slammed the door on his way out. She heard the tires screech as he peeled out of the drive. Jain had that awful feeling again. Something bad was going to happen, and she was powerless to stop it.

She wanted to cry.

Chapter 10

Jain slept fitfully that night. She tossed and turned as she dreamed one dream after another. The dreams were so real. She could feel the danger. Someone was trying to kill her. A dark, shadowy, man with no face stood with his gun pointed at her chest. There was no place to run and no place to hide. They were in this big open area. She saw his finger on the trigger. As he started to squeeze, a man in a dark blue uniform stepped up from nowhere and was suddenly between her and the man with the gun. He was holding a large metal shield. She could hear the gunfire. She could hear the bullets ping as the shield deflected them and they bounced harmlessly to the ground. She awoke shaking with fear. It had been so real. When morning finally arrived, she felt like she hadn't slept at all. She was working days this week, and she had to get the kids off to school. It was a real effort, and she had that awful feeling that something bad was going to happen.

When she got to work, she met Ray's friend Bill, coming out the door with a cup of coffee. "Old Ray's on his way to Texas again. I saw him leaving out about an hour ago. He won't be back until Friday."

"Good." Jain felt like telling him that she didn't care or that she wished he'd take Roni and stay there, but she knew better than to say it. She kept on walking.

At break, she tried to talk to Lisa about her dreams and her premonitions, but Lisa didn't want to hear it.

"Please spare me the dreams and the prophecy bit, Jain. You are just letting things get to you. We knew that Roni would cause more problems when you sent her home early. If she is not pregnant, we ought to beat her. We need to teach her a lesson."

"Someone tried that before, remember? Remember that social worker and what a mess that was? I think I'll just leave her alone."

The awful feeling that something bad was going to happen stayed with Jain, but she kept it to herself. The feeling was so strong, that when she was alone, she cried.

Rumors were flying at work. Bill was worried about Roni. He said that she was keeping bad company. Her neighbors were calling the police station and reporting her several times a night. She was having wild parties and disturbing the peace. Jim was almost arrested for fighting with one of her houseguests. Jain came in early and heard Bill telling the midnight staff how he 'felt responsible for that girl.' Ray wasn't due back for three more days. Roni's aunt and uncle were supposed to come and visit. They lived in Texas. Roni had stayed with them when she was younger. Maybe they would help.

Jim came by at lunch and talked to Lisa. He told Lisa that Roni had a new boyfriend. He said that he remembered how Lisa used to worry about Roni, and that he was afraid she was headed for trouble. He feared that she would get hurt.

"I sure do hope so!" Lisa had blurted and Jim got mad and left.

Jain played with the food on her plate as Lisa paced and ranted. They were the only two left in the dinning room.

"She turns their brains to mush! Jim used to have a brain. How does she do that? He actually thinks I ought to care what happens to her! I wish she were dead! I wish he were dead! The nerve of that man! He must be on drugs!"

Lisa wound down and sat at the table with Jain. She propped her elbows on the table and held her head in her hands. “This is unreal. I feel like I’m in a nightmare and can’t wake up. You’re the only person who knows what is going on. Everyone else thinks that I’m crazy or that I’m making all this up. Sometimes, I think I’ve lost my mind. All I want is to have my life back.”

Jain felt like she was carrying the weight of the world on her shoulders. She thought about Lisa and Jim. She thought about her own life and she thought about Ray. She thought about Roni and her new boyfriend. She was sure that he was married to someone else. Roni wouldn’t be interested if he weren’t. She wondered what Ray would do if he knew. She remembered his temper and she wondered if he still kept a gun. She thought about her dreams of the man with the gun. Was that what the dream was about? Would Ray blame her and try to kill her for real? She tossed and turned in her bed and could not sleep. She wasn't sure that she cared. She dreaded the dreams.

She was tired Thursday morning when she dragged herself to work. It had been a rough week and it wouldn't be over until the next Monday. It was her weekend to work and the kids were going on a short trip with her sister. They left this morning to visit with relatives in another state. It was the first days of school that they had missed in over a year. Jain almost didn't let them go. She had that strong sense of foreboding again. She tried everything to shake it. She reminded herself that Ray would be back tomorrow and that he would more than likely be around causing trouble, especially with this new Roni business. At least the kids would be spared that. To keep her mind occupied,

Jain spent her spare time working on her new home. She was able to do a lot of the work herself and the kids had even helped with the painting and stuff. They could move in within a month. The only thing that worried Jain, was that they would be more isolated. She convinced herself that it might be a good thing. They would be further away from Ray and Roni. Maybe they'd be safer that way. Neighbors never wanted to get involved anyway.

The day started off slow. There were only a few patients and Jain was glad. They even had plenty of help today. Jain passed meds and caught up on paper work. It was only nine am and she was already bored. The ward clerk was lost in her own thoughts and the quiet was unreal. The sudden blare of the scanner made Jain jump. At almost the same time that the scanner came alive, she heard the sirens start up. She caught bits of conversation over the scanner. "Shots fired!" "We need the ambulance!" "Hurry!"

She looked out the window of an empty room as two police cars and the ambulance screamed past the hospital. They were headed east on West Main, toward the other side of town. They couldn't have gone far, because the sirens stopped suddenly instead of fading away in the distance. Jain got prepared. She and Lisa headed for the E R and checked the crash cart, the I V supply, the O2, dressing supplies, and everything else. Gunshots could mean just about anything. They waited, not knowing what was coming in. The doctor arrived and waited with them. He had heard the sirens and knew that he would be needed at the hospital.

"What's going on? Do we know anything yet?"

"Only that shots were fired and the police and the ambulance are on the scene. I thought they'd be here by now" Jain looked out the ER door. "It must be bad."

"Maybe no one was hurt." The doctor looked hopeful.

"I don't Know - -,"

"Jain!" Lisa interrupted. "Don't start with the gloom and the doom!"

The doctor looked from one to the other of them until Lisa told him about Jain's premonitions. He had no time to comment about it, because they heard the sirens getting closer. Jain knew it was bad, if they were too busy to make radio contact. As she looked out the door, the ambulance wheeled into the parking lot. They took the turn so fast that Jain thought that it was going to turn over. Both police cars came right behind the ambulance. Lights were flashing and sirens screaming on all vehicles. The person on the gurney was covered with blood. A policeman had been driving and both EMTs were in back of the unit, trying to stop the bleeding by applying pressure. An IV was going wide open. Jain quickly started another one. They typed and cross-matched, for two units of blood. Lisa paged the nurses' station to call in the surgery crew. They were there within minutes. The patient was covered with blood, but it was all coming from the chest and abdomen. Jain grabbed the pour top saline and started cleaning and sponging, the clothing had already been cut away. When they found the source, Lisa was suctioning and retracting and the doctor was already clamping off and suturing bleeders. Jain hung two units of blood, piggy backing them into the IV's, running everything wide open. Everyone was shouting, the doctor barking orders.

“Is there a pulse?”

“Very weak.”

“What about blood pressure?”

“60 palpated.”

The anesthesioligist and the surgery crew arrived and they started wheeling the patient to OR. For the first time, Jain really looked at the patient and saw who it was. She turned white and leaned against the wall. She saw all the frantic attempts to save the life in slow motion. She looked past the patient for the first time and straight into the smirking face of Roni Davis, who stood there in bloody cloths, eyes shinning.

“Jain! Get with it! Get that IV pole!” The doctor snapped. “We’ve got to get him into OR now!”

They were running, pushing the cart toward the OR. Jain followed pushing the two IV poles. Lisa was on the cart, checking vital signs and holding pressure.

As they wheeled him through the double doors of the OR and the anesthesiologist took over the IVs, Jain heard Lisa say "Zero blood pressure."

Jain slumped to the floor. The patient on that gurney was Ray! Still stunned, she took a few deep breaths and then stood on wobbly knees. It would be a miracle if Ray survived. She started praying for one. Lisa came out of OR.

"Jain, what on earth happened to you? You are whiter than your uniform!"

"Lisa, that patient is Ray."

"Oh My God!" Lisa supported Jain as they slowly walked back toward the ER. Lisa hadn't looked close enough to identify him when they were so busy trying to save his life either. Now she didn't know what to say. Half way down the hall, they met Bill.

"Jain, we need you down here. Roni is covered with blood. I don't know if she's hurt or not. That other guy has a shoe full of blood. I think Roni is in shock. She keeps babbling about Ray coming home early. He was supposed to be in Texas."

Jain stopped and stared at him. She opened her mouth, but nothing came out. She went into the nearest bathroom and washed her face in cold water. Lisa followed. Slowly, she returned to reality. "That man is crazy. The whole world is crazy. Does he even know that Ray will most likely die? How much more damage can Roni do? How many more will suffer?"

It hit them both at the same time. "Jim!"

They ran after Bill. "Was anyone else there? Was anyone else hurt?"

"I just told you, Jain, Roni —,"

"Forget Roni! Was anyone else at the scene? Did you see Jim? Lisa needs to know."

Bill looked bewildered. Jain went to talk to the other officer. He told her that there were only the three people on the scene when they arrived. Neighbors had called in and reported hearing gunshots. They'd called earlier about the noise, and said that Roni was having a wild party. They had more urgent calls to take care of first, and had not responded until the gunshots were reported. Witnesses reported that a lot of people left soon after Ray arrived. They heard a lot of yelling, then they heard the shots. No eyewitness to the act.

"Go and call Jim, I'll take care of this." Jain put on fresh gloves and removed the shoe. The man winced, but didn't say a word. She cleaned the wound. The bleeding had almost stopped. It looked like the bullet went all the way through. She found the entrance and exit wounds. She sent the man to Xray to be sure there were no broken bones, then she packed the wound with sterile 4x4s wet with sterile NS, and applied dry, sterile dressings over that. She gave him a tetanus shot. The aide had come down and done the paper work while they were working on Ray. This man and Roni were both wearing handcuffs and state troopers were now on the scene. Jain turned to Roni. As she checked her over, she wanted to strangle her. She couldn't help it. She feared that Ray wouldn't survive and she would have to tell her kids that their dad was dead. Silently, she prayed for him and for help for herself. Suddenly it dawned on her. The premonitions and the dreams! This was what it was all about. She thanked God that she and the kids were safe and protected. It could have been them.

"Jain, can't you clean all this yucky blood off of me?" Roni was actually enjoying this. Jain looked her in the eye and didn't say a word. She got a wet cloth and cleaned the blood away. The state troopers had already made photos. There wasn't a scratch on her.

Lisa was furious when she came back into the room. "What did you do to him? He can't even talk." She stepped toward Roni and Roni took a step backward. Jain moved between them. A trooper spoke to Bill, and he came over to stand beside Roni.

Bill placed his hand on Roni's elbow. "Sorry, Roni, we have to take you down to the station. I'm sure this will all be straightened out soon."

Everyone left and house keeping came to clean up the mess. Jain was almost in shock as she watched them clean up Ray's blood. There was so much of it. When the shift ended, Ray was still in surgery. His mom and one of his brothers were in the waiting room. They just looked at Jain and Lydia burst out crying. She tried to comfort them, but she couldn't give them much hope. She had no answers to their questions. She knew that somehow, they blamed her for this. Ray probably would too, if he lived.

Ray was in surgery for hours. The shift changed and they were short of help. Jain continued to work. She had to stay busy. She would work twenty-four hours straight before she could go home.

When the surgery was finally done, they put Ray in the special care room and two nurses stayed with him. He still had the two IV's and the foley catheter. He was on the respirator. Now, he also had drain tubes and dressings that were having to be reinforced often. They were still having to apply pressure to stop the bleeding at times. He was whiter than the sheets. They let his mother and brother in to see him for just a moment. Her son and a nurse were supporting Lydia when she came out. The doctor looked exhausted. He spoke briefly to the family, then went to the doctors' lounge. Jain knew that he wouldn't leave. He'd stay in the hospital all night. She couldn't either. The crisis had made them short staffed on midnights as well.

After working for twenty-four straight hours, she dragged herself home and fell into the bed, still not knowing if Ray would live or die. She thought about calling the kids, but what would she tell them? She drifted into a fretful sleep. Six hours later, the ringing of the phone woke her. It was the hospital calling her back to work.

"Is Ray still alive?"

"Yes, but he's still bad." It was Dana on the phone. "I can't special him. I'm not up to it."

"I know, Jain, We all do. We just need an RN on the floor. We'll get you plenty of help. I'd stay over if I could, but there's no one to stay with Mom." Dana's mom was bedbound. Dana wouldn't put her in the Nursing Home. She hired a sitter when she was at work and she took care of her the rest of the time. Dana was an only child.

Jain got in the shower and ran the water as hot as she could stand it. She made a pot of strong coffee and drank two cups. She realized that she hadn't eaten in over thirty-six hours, and managed to eat half a bowl of soup and a few crackers. She was still shaky, but she dressed and went to work.

"You don't have to do anything but just be here, Jain. You've got plenty of help and we've only got ten patients, except for Ray. He's the only one that's bad. He's doing a little better. It looks like he just might make it if no more complications develop." Dana proceeded to give her a report on Ray's condition. "Can you believe it? One little bullet did all that damage. It entered the abdomen, traveled upward and got the spleen, barely missed his heart, and did some damage to his left lung. They had to remove his spleen. He's got a colostomy. That may be temporary, we don't know for sure. He lost part of his left lung. They are trying to wean him off the respirator. His mom and two brothers are camped out in the waiting room."

Jain had another cup of coffee, made rounds, and finally, went to the waiting room to talk to Lydia. She took a pot of coffee and some cups. They all looked up with questioning eyes.

"I just thought you might like some coffee. There's no change in Ray's condition"

"Thanks, Jain." This came from Dave. The other two didn't speak.

Jain poured a cup of coffee and offered it to Lydia.

For a moment, it looked like she wouldn't take it, then she took a sip and glared at Jain. "This is all your fault! Somehow I know it is. You have killed my son." She dissolved into tears.

"Mom!" Dave was on his feet. At first he was angry, then he looked at his mom and sat beside her. "You know the police told you that Jain wasn't there. She was at work when it happened. Ray has been headed for trouble for a long time. We all tried to tell him about Roni." He wrapped both arms around his Mom and buried his head in her shoulder.

Lydia looked at Jain. "I guess I know you didn't do it, but I just can't believe that you are a real nurse. You are just like me. You sewed in the same factory that I did. You came from a family that had less than we did. You have got above your raising, Jain. You have no business out here talking to doctors and telling other people what to do. That Dana told me you helped save Ray's life, but I don't believe that. You should be home with your children or working at the factory."

Dave raised his head and starred at his Mom, then he got up and walked away.

"All I ever wanted was to be a wife and a mother to my children, but it didn't work out that way. I love my children, Lydia, and I used to love Ray. My kids are happy now. We had it hard when Ray left. I'm glad that I was able to give them a better life. Ray doesn't know what he missed. I feel sorry for him. I'm sorry for what you're going through. Let me know if I can help you in anyway." Exasperated, Jain got up and went back to work.

It was quiet on the floor and Jain was restless. She checked on the patients until they complained about it. She went to the dinning room and drank coffee until it made her nervous. Bill came by, complaining that they still had Roni and her friend in jail.

"I'll be glad when Ray gets able to tell them what happened and make them let Roni go. That man, Jake, he probably had a hand in it. I don't know what Roni sees in him. I can't help it if he is her friend, he's bad news. I don't trust him and I don't know why he's so interested in you, Jain. It's a nightmare."

Jain sat there with her mouth open. Don't you understand that Ray might not make it? She wanted to scream this at Bill. Roni may have killed him. My whole life has been a nightmare since I first heard of Roni. It's a constant battle not to hate her, and sometimes I loose the battle. It was catching up to her;

sleep deprivation, the harassment, Lydia's insults, worry, and exhaustion. She zoned out.

"Jain, Jain, what's wrong with you?" She was vaguely aware of Bill's voice.

"Bill! Don't you need to go check on Roni or something?" Jain wasn't even aware that Lisa had come into the room. She wasn't even working tonight.

"Yeah, I guess I'd better. No one else seems to care about her." He got up and left. He gave Jain a funny look as he went through the door. "Tell old Ray that I asked about him."

Lisa put her hands on Jain's shoulders. "Come on, we need to get some fresh air."

"I can't leave, I'm the only R.N. in the building—"

"We're just going to step outside. You shouldn't have to be here at all and I told them that. I found out some of what happened. You know these halls have ears."

"Lydia blames me"

"What else is new? She deserves to have Roni for a daughter in law. How did you ever put up with her?"

"Lisa, you found out what happened? Did Roni shoot Ray?"

"No, Jake did it, but sweet little Roni had a hand in it. Jim was there. He saw it all. They were having a party. Jim thought he was Roni's date. I bet all the men there thought that. Anyway, Roni went upstairs to use the bathroom. She was gone for a long time and Jim didn't know many of the people there, so he went up to look for her. He went to the bathroom first, and found it empty. Being anxious gives him diareaha, so he had to use the john. While he did that, Ray came home unexpected, and the people downstairs scattered. Jim heard the commotion. He heard Ray yelling for the guests to leave, the cars peeling out, and then Ray's footsteps coming up the stairs. He said his first thoughts were for Roni's safety." Lisa winced.

"What did he do?"

"He opened the door and listened. He heard moans and noise coming from Roni's bedroom. He saw Ray at the top of the stairs, so he didn't know what was happening. When Ray went and yanked open the bedroom door, Jim followed him. The bed was against the far wall, but Ray had already reached the foot of it. Jim said that he was frozen there, looking through the open door way. It was like watching a movie in slow motion. He saw the gun lying on the bedside table, but he couldn't say a word. He said he tried, but no sound would come out. He heard Ray curse, then he saw Roni look back at him and smile. He said that's when

Jake picked up the gun and fired it at Ray. The explosion startled Roni and she reached for the gun that was still in Jake's hand. The gun went off again, hitting Jake in the foot. Ray lay crumpled on the floor, his blood already pooling around him. That's when Jim ran downstairs and out the back door. He said that it felt like he vomited for hours. Someone must have heard the shots and called the police, because he heard the sirens and saw the flashing lights coming down the road. He panicked and ran. That's why he couldn't talk when I called him from the ER."

"You mean Ray came home and found Roni in bed with another man? I don't understand."

"What don't you understand? You know what a tramp Roni is."

"But if they were making love —-, Lisa, the bullet angled up. You know the entry site was his abdomen, then it went up to his spleen and his lung. But you said Roni didn't shoot him. Even if the bed was very low on the floor —-"

"Oh, I see," Lisa started laughing. "Jain, sometimes I forget how innocent you can be. Jain, Roni was on top. Jake was flat of his back and Ray was towering over them at the foot of the bed."

"Oh." That was all Jain could say as the picture began to form in her mind. She sat with her back against the brick building of the hospital. She couldn't laugh. It would be another scandal that she and her kids would have to live down. There would be no way to keep it from the children. Some cruel person would be sure to tell them. It was always something. Once again, she wished she could just move away. Oh well, the house was finally finished. She would keep the kids occupied with moving. Surely they were safe now, with Ray in the hospital and Roni in jail.

"Jain? I'm sorry, I've upset you. I just thought you'd want to know, besides, if I didn't tell you, someone else would. Jain, please don't be mad. I didn't mean to hurt you." Lisa shook her gently. "Jain?"

"No." She sighed and looked at Lisa. "I'm not as good a person as you think I am. I was being selfish. We don't even know yet if Ray is going to live and I was thinking about what all this will do to my kids. I was thinking about how it will complicate our lives. I've been mad and upset at Lydia for putting me down when her son may be dying. When did I become so self centered? I'll be at the altar Sunday. You know what? I was even dreading facing the people at church, making excuses not to go. I'm a mess. I've not done anything for anyone tonight. I need to sleep and talk to my kids. I need to really talk to God."

"There you are! We've been looking for you. It's about time to give report. We wrote everything down for you. Oh, Ray is trying to talk. They may take him off the respirator tomorrow." Mary handed Jain a sheet of paper and went back inside.

Jain dragged herself to the dinning room and gave the worst report of her life. Then she went to check on Ray.

"He's asking for Roni." The nurse shook her head. "We just told him that she wasn't here right now. His Mom is pleased that he's awake."

Jain went to the waiting room. "Lydia, I'm sorry that I didn't think to offer before, but you are all welcome to stay at my house so you'll be close to Ray if you want to. I'm going home now. I've only slept about six hours since this happened."

"No thank you, Jain, I wouldn't feel welcome. I don't know how you can sleep at all." Lydia turned her back and walked to the window. Her sons surrounded her and she leaned onto Dave's shoulder and Jain went home.

She opened the door and the dog met her with an empty bowl in its mouth. Jain knelt down on her knees. "Jill, I'm so sorry." She fed and watered the dog. The poor dog had used the newspaper for a bathroom and Jain cleaned up the mess and sprayed room deodorizer. She opened the back door and hit the shower. When she came out, she went straight to her bed and fell across it. She started to pray, but fell asleep. When she awoke the next morning, the sun was shinning through the window and Jill was snuggled in her arms. Just for a minute, she panicked when she saw that the front door was unlocked and the back door was standing open, but then she remembered that she had left them that way. Nothing was out of place. There was no obscene writing on the house. All was quiet. Jain checked the calendar and turned on the TV to be sure what day it was. It was almost noon. The kids would be home tomorrow. She would have to tell them about Ray. She called the hospital to see how he was doing. Thank God he was still better. She waited while the ward clerk checked the schedule to see if she still had the next two days off. When she hung up, she unplugged the phone so that they couldn't call her in to work. She needed to rest and to think. She cooked herself and Jill a really big breakfast, then started packing the things they used the least into boxes. She had to stay busy.

She jumped when she heard a car pull into the drive and was disappointed to see Bill in his police car. She was not going in to work today. She just couldn't. She told him so when she went to the door.

"Oh no, Jain, that's not why I'm here. I'm sorry you thought that. I wanted to talk to you about Roni. Ray wants to see her, but they won't let her out of jail to go see him. I've never seen anything like it. Those FBI guys have just taken over. It beats all I've ever seen. They are camped out at Roni's and Jake's cells and won't even let them have visitors. They won't even let me talk to Roni. I know that poor girl is scared out of her mind. They act like she's a hardened criminal or something. I thought maybe you could talk to them." He paced back and forth in the yard and rubbed his head as he said all this.

Jain could feel the anger rising inside her. Just before she exploded and went off on Bill, it registered. FBI? She didn't know the FBI was involved. Lisa hadn't said anything about that. The fog that had surrounded her for the past few days began to lift. She had lots of questions. She would control her anger and talk to Bill. Why would the FBI be involved?

"Bill, Roni almost got Ray killed. He almost died. He still might. How much more of a criminal could she be?"

"Now Jain, you know she wouldn't do that. Why are you so hard on her? It was just an accident, just a domestic squabble. Poor Roni, it seems like her friends are all gone when she needs them the most."

It was useless. Jain tried to get him off the subject of Roni. "Why is the FBI involved with this? Did something else happen that I haven't heard about?"

“I don’t know. They won’t tell me a thing. They only talk to the chief. I heard that they’ve been asking all kinds of questions about Ray and Roni and even you. They checked into all the complaints that were called in when you and Ray got divorced and they pulled the records from that accident when that woman from out of town was killed. You remember, the one they thought was you? It’s ridiculous if you ask me. They’ve got chains on Jake, even when he’s in that cell. His wife is here, but they won’t let her in to see him. She’s staying with Roni’s parents. Turns out, she’s Roni’s mother’s sister. That would make Jake her uncle. I knew all the time that the stuff people are telling wasn’t true. Roni wouldn’t have been in bed with her uncle. Will you talk to them, Jain?”

“What? No. Whether you know it or not, Bill, Roni is where she needs to be. She is dangerous. I don’t know how you can be so blind. You are supposed to be Ray's friend. He's going to need his friends now."

"Well, just be that way, Jain. I should have known that you wouldn't help. I don't know why, I just thought you might understand." He got in his car and left.

Jain called Lisa. "Did you know about the FBI?"

"Not until this morning. They took Jim in for questioning. I guess you aren't so paranoid after all, Jain, but I don't know what all is going on. The news reporters from Nashville just got into town. I saw the van in front of the jail. I guess we'll know soon enough. I'll call you back after I talk to Jim again."

Jain was restless. Jill wouldn't leave her side. Unable to sit still, she started loading things into the car and moving them to her new house. The dog made every trip with her. By the end of the day, all that was left was the TV and the big stuff and her brother was coming with his truck Monday morning to help her with that. Once again, she fell into an exhausted sleep and didn't move until early the next morning when she was awakened by the sound of a car in the drive. She grabbed her robe and ran to the door, but Jill was already there, wiggling all over. Jain opened the door and gathered her children into her arms.

Brenda took one look and said, "What have they done now?"

"Come and sit down, Bren." Jain went to the kitchen and started the coffee. She got out the milk and cereal as they all sat around the kitchen table. She put a hand on the shoulder of each of her children. "Ray is in the hospital, but I think he's going to be ok." She was surprised when the kids said nothing and just started eating.

"What's wrong with him?" Brenda asked the question. "That coffee smells good."

"He was shot."

"Really? Did Roni do it?"

"No, her friend did."

"Friend, huh?"

Jain said, "Kids, I'll take you to the hospital to see him when you get through eating, ok?"

"Sure."

"Ok"

They continued to eat and give bites to Jill. Jain wondered if they understood. She tried again. "Kids, he's pretty sick. I hope you won't be too upset."

"Ok, Mom, get dressed and we'll go to the hospital." Cass kicked Stan's leg under the table when he started to protest.

"Call me with all the details later." Brenda said as she headed for the door. "I'm taking my coffee with me."

Jain went with her kids into the room to see Ray. He really looked better today. The walked slowly up to the side of the bed. "Hi Ray, how are you feeling?" Cass asked.

"Hi Ray," echoed Stan.

"Hi, I don't feel too good." Then they were all silent. It was as if they were strangers. He doesn't even know how to talk to his own children, what a shame, Jain thought. She had been worried that the kids would be upset, but now she found herself feeling sorry for Ray. He doesn't even know what he's missing, she thought.

After they stood there for a few minutes, the kids looked at their mother. Their looks plainly said that they had done their duty and wanted to leave. Jain was at a loss. She was wondering what to do next when Stan looked at her and said, "Can we go now?"

"Yeah, I'm sure Ray needs to rest. I'll bring you back later."

"Bye Ray, hope you feel better soon." Cass was heading for the door.

"Yeah, bye Ray." Stan was right behind his sister.

They were half way down the hall when Jain left the room, eager to get out of the hospital. Jain watched as they almost ran smack into Lydia. As she walked toward them, she saw Lydia bend toward them and reach out her hands. The kids looked at each other and backed away.

"You don't even know who I am, do you? You poor things. It's not your fault, it' Jain's. I'm your grandmother. My, how you've grown."

"We know who you are, you're Ray's mother." Cass said this as she took Stan's hand and they started to go on down the hall.

"Wait. You call your father Ray? What has that woman been telling you? Your father is a good man. This mess is all Jain's fault. You used to call him daddy."

Jain quickened her steps. Her body tensed. She would not let Lydia do this to her children, no matter how hurt she must be. As she drew nearer, she was surprised to find that her kids could stand up for themselves.

"We haven't had a daddy in a long time. We haven't seen you either. We know what happened and Mom didn't tell us. We went to see Ray only because she wanted us to. We're going now." Cass waited for Lydia to step aside.

"I would have come to see you, but Jain wouldn't let me." Lydia reached out again, but the kids backed away. "She won't even let your father see you."

"That's not true. She always lets Ray in." Cass took Stan's hand and pulled him down the hall.

"Don't say mean things about our Mom!" Stan tossed this over his shoulder.

They didn't notice Jain frozen in her tracks ten feet behind them.

The ride home was silent. They arrived just before noon and turned on the TV. Jain had not had the electricity turned off. It was in the landlords' name, so it hadn't been a problem to get it at her new house. The kids groaned as a special news bulletin interrupted the program.

'We interrupt this program to bring you breaking news from the small town of Hohenwald,

located about a hundred miles south west of here. Law officials and the FBI have taken one of the ten most wanted criminals in the United States into custody for attempted murder. Jake Morlon has been on the FBI's ten most wanted list for seven years. He's wanted for murder in five different states. Circumstances of his arrest are still unclear, but he was arrested and jailed in Hohenwald a few nights ago for attempted murder. The name of the victim is not being released to protect the family. The victim's wife was also arrested in connection with the crime. Jake Morlon is being extradited to Texas to stand trial there, since most of the crimes he committed were done there. We repeat, Jake Morlon, one of the FBI's ten most wanted has been captured. Stay tuned for further information as it develops."

Jake's picture and the news logo flashed across the screen. Jain and the kids stared at the screen with open mouths. Jill's hair rose and she growled as they showed Jake's picture once more. It suddenly occurred to Jain just how miraculous it was that she and the children were alive and well. She remembered all the dreams she'd had of someone trying to kill her and of her protector. She thanked God with all her heart.

She was glad that they were taking Jake out of the state. She wished that they would take Roni with him, but she knew that they wouldn't. She would have a trial, though, because of all the publicity, they couldn't just let her go. For the first time, Jain was glad that everything was out in the open. Lisa called with more details. The FBI had matched the bullet from Jake's gun to the one that had killed that woman from out of town who had been driving the blue car that was so much like Jain's. Two agents were still in town. They were going to question Ray and Jain. Lisa thought they would get to her also. The rumor was that Jake had killed that woman, believing that she was Jain. They thought that someone, maybe Roni or Ray had hired him to do it. Rumors were wild. Everyone had an opinion about what had happened.

It had to be Roni, Jain thought this as she remembered the time that someone put sugar in Ray's gas tank when he was in Texas. When she was questioned, she told the agent everything that she could remember. Ray, of course, told them that everything was Jain's fault. Someone must have agreed with Jain, because Roni was charged with conspiracy to commit murder and attempted murder. There were other charges, but no one knew what they were. She was going to trial and it was big news. The reporters from

Nashville were going to cover it. Bill was outraged. He was interviewed on television and was featured on the news, saying, "That girl is innocent. She didn't do this." Ray also came to her defense. He still didn't know all the details, and he thought that Roni was being accused of trying to kill him. He told the police that he shot himself. He didn't know there was a witness and didn't know about the evidence that had been collected. As soon as he got out of the hospital, he hired her a lawyer. He was still very weak, but he promised to be by her side at the trial.

Sunday came and Jain and the kids went to church. She needed to be fed with the word of God, to feel His loving spirit wash over her and revitalize her soul. She made a special effort not to arrive early. She tried to slip in quietly and sit down on the back row, but the preacher's wife must have been watching for her. She came and gave Jain and the kids a hug. “Jain, we’ve been praying for you. We had a special service and we had some members to pray every day, for you and the kids and for Ray’s recovery.”

“Thank you.” It seemed inadequate, but Jain didn’t know what else to say. Lots of people just smiled at her or gave her a pat on the shoulder. It was time for church to start. They sang a couple of songs and the preacher led them in prayer. As the prayer ended, Jain was aware that someone had squeezed onto the pew beside her. When she opened her eyes, she wanted to sink down under the seat. Brad smiled and squeezed her hand. She concentrated on the sermon. She concentrated on every word that the preacher spoke. At first it was awkward, but then she felt the Spirit begin to fill the church and seep into her soul. Soon, she wasn’t even aware of who was sitting beside her.

When they gave the altar call, she went forward. She had known all week that she needed to do it, that she needed God's help to get rid of the mean and selfish feelings that had sneaked up on her. Words that came from the depth her heart poured out of her mouth and tears streamed down her cheeks and soaked the altar. Church members gathered around to help her pray. She didn't care. She confessed all her sins and begged for forgiveness. She asked God for wisdom and for strength. When she got up from the altar, she knew that she had received that and more. She felt clean again and was no longer carrying around the guilt that she had felt for all the bad thoughts and feelings that she'd had about Ray, Roni, and Lydia. She looked around for the kids and saw that they were with Brad and the girl that he was usually with on Sunday. She headed in that direction. She wasn't going to be a coward today. She was so grateful for her church family. She realized that she was also grateful for her blood related family and everything else that God had given her. In spite of everything, she was blessed and she would try not to forget that.

"Hi Jain, we're so glad that you're ok." The pretty woman gave her a hug. It wasn't a fake hug; you could actually feel how much this woman cared about people. Love and peace surrounded her like a physical presence. "We've been praying for you. I tried to fast, but I'm not good at that. I'm Jamie."

"Thank you." Jain smiled.

"You're a greedy pig, that's what you are! You ate all of the blueberry pie! Every single crumb!" Brad punched Jamie playfully on the shoulder. "You didn't even leave me a bite. Hi, Jain."

"Guilty." Jamie laughed. "It's why I broke the fast. I couldn't resist the pie. But Brad, you fasted for two days."

"Jain, can we have dinner together?" Brad asked. "We need to talk."

"Thanks, but I can't, I- -" Her newly found courage was weakening.

"I'll watch the kids for you. I owe Brad a favor anyway, and I love kids." Jamie interrupted. "I'm good with kids, you can ask anyone."

"It's not that, I have to work evening shift today. I have to go now, or I'll be late for work. Thanks for everything. You have no idea how much I appreciate it. There aren't words adequate enough to express how much it means to me." Jain herded the kids to the car and hurried home. She had to rush to get the kids to her mother's house and get ready to go to work. In the morning, she planned to finish the moving. They would finally be in their new home. It wouldn't take long. Surely they would be safe now.

Ray was out of special care. All the tubes were gone. He was insisting that he needed to go home. He needed to be with Roni. Even if she was in jail, he wanted to be able to see her and talk to her. The doctor agreed to let him go in a few more days, if he would get his mother to stay with him. He'd have to come to the office every other day to have his dressing changed and he'd have to learn how to do his own colostomy care. Jain was relieved that he was going to be all right. Even the colostomy was temporary.

Roni's trial would start soon. She'd been bound over to grand jury. Lots of people had been called in for witnesses. It was still the talk of the town. It looked like Roni would have to pay this time. There were numerous charges against her. One of them was harboring a dangerous criminal. Jake was gone and security was less severe now, but Roni was still locked up without bail. Bill was having fit on top of fit, but he couldn't get her out of jail. It seemed that he was more worried about Roni than he was about Ray. The district attorney had asked Jain to be available for the trial. He wanted her in the courtroom. She agreed, partly because she had days built up that she had to take off or loose the time, and partly because she wanted to know what was going on and why Roni and Ray had put her and the kids through so much the past few years. Mostly, she just wanted closure. She wanted to understand and she just wanted it over. The constant strain and worry was getting to her. The last time she had completely relaxed was when she and the kids had gone to the mountains. Now that seemed so long ago.

Even then, she'd come home to find that someone had died and people had thought that it was Jain.

Chapter 11

Jain and the kids finished the moving. They were finally home! In their new house, with each having a room of their own. Everyone was happy, even Jill and the cats.

They had been concerned about the cats, someone had told them that cats wouldn't move, that they would leave and try to go back to their previous home. Not these cats, they checked out every corner and closet in the house, then they crawled into a large paper bag and went to sleep. Jill checked the place over inside and out, even going off into the woods. The children were afraid that she'd get lost until Jain reminded them that the place was fenced in. Even with the fence, Jain watched out the window or sat on the porch when the kids were outside. Everyone said she was overprotective. She sometimes wondered if she'd be able to let them go when they were all grown up and ready to live their own lives. She didn't want to think about it. Instead, she thought about the new house, the yard, all the space, and her children playing with the dog, having the time of their lives. She started to relax a little.

At first, it felt strange to have so many days off at once, but now it felt good. The phone was still not working, but she visited her family almost every day. She didn't go by the hospital. If she was needed there or at the trial, the police could always come and tell her. On Wednesday night, she thought about going to church, but she just didn't have the energy. She felt relaxed and lazy. She even put the grocery shopping off until Friday. It had to be done then, they were about out of everything, and the kids were beginning to complain about not liking the meals that she put before them. The hungry years forgotten, they were getting quite picky about what they wanted to eat. Spoiled kids! Once she had feared that they would starve to death, now she was so thankful for what they had.

They left Jill in the yard when they went shopping. It felt odd, not having to leave her in the house or take her with them. She stood at the gate and whined when they fastened her inside the yard. The shopping seamed to take forever and cost a fortune. As the teenage boy eyed Cass and loaded the bags into the car, Lisa pulled up and got out of her car.

"Jain! There was a man that came to the hospital looking for you yesterday. What a hunk! He seemed really worried about you. Mary told him where you live. I tried to call you and see if that was ok, but your phone must be out of order."

"Yeah, it's supposed to be fixed Monday. We've been kind of taking a break from the world. The only people I've seem for the past week were family. It sure felt good. Was that guy from the DAs office, do you think? The trial was not supposed to start until Monday. I really dread that, but I'll be glad to get it over with and finally know why all this stuff happened." From the corner of her eye, Jain saw Cass smile at the grocery store boy and Stan make a face.

"I don't know, he wasn't wearing a suit. He had on blue jeans and a plaid shirt. He had gorgeous eyes and wonderful hair. I bet he was over six feet tall." Lisa had a dreamy look in her eyes that made Jain smile.

"He sure made an impression on you."

"Oh, not just me! You should have heard the others gushing over him. You know how Sandy is." Lisa mimicked her; *"Humph! Wonder what he wants with*

Jain!" Mary just stood there with her eyes wide. Even the doctor wanted to know who he was and why he was asking for you. I think you've been holding out on me, Jain. I bet that you didn't find that guy at church." Lisa went toward the store entrance.

Now Jain was really curious. Surely Roni couldn't be causing more problems from jail. Ray was still too weak and too worried about Roni to think about anything like that. She didn't feel any apprehension. It must have something to do with the trial. Brenda thought that they had now charged Roni with murder. She was talking about it yesterday. Probably just someone the district attorney sent over to the hospital to remind her to show up in court. Jain started the car and headed for home.

She slowed down to stop and open the gate, but saw that it was already open. She drove through, telling the kids to stay in the car. The unfinished sentence died on her lips as she saw Brad sitting on the porch, dangling his legs. Jill was next to him, her head in his lap. What happened to the dog who didn't like men? Jain couldn't believe what she was seeing. The kids jumped out of the car and ran to the porch.

"Hey! Jill likes Brad! You are the only man that she has ever liked. Look, Mom." Cass was a regular chatterbox.

"Didn't she try to bite you?" Stan wanted to know.

"Well, no. Jill had a problem when I got here. I helped her out and now we're buddies, aren't we girl?" Jill wagged her stub and snuggled closer to Brad.

"What kind of a problem?"

"Well, she must have tried to follow you when you left. She had her head stuck between the gate and the fence. The gate must have given a little when she pushed on it and she got her head through, but her body got stuck and when she tried to pull her head back, the gate wouldn't give to the inside like it did to the outside. She was stuck pretty good. She was hot and tired. I knew her name from hearing you talk about her and I had some water in the car. I just talked to her and gave her some water. When she started to trust me a little, I opened the gate. I petted her a little to calm her down, but now I think she just likes the petting. I needed to talk to your mom, so I sat here and kept her company. I hope that's ok."

"Kids, get the groceries out of the car." Now Jain knew who the hunk was.

"Don't be mad, Jain, I was worried half to death. I went to the house where you used to live and found it empty. I was about to panic. I was going to go to the police, but Jamie told me to try the hospital instead."

Brad helped them take the bags inside and continued to talk. He told her that there were further charges against Roni. He didn't know if this had just happened or if it had just been kept quiet until now. Roni was charged with the murder of that woman who was shot in the head awhile back. People were saying that Jake was driving the truck and that Roni did the shooting. Jain wasn't all that surprised. She remembered that when it had happened, she thought that it was Ray and Roni trying to kill her. She could tell that Brad expected her to be more upset, maybe he thought she was in shock, because he kept looking at her. She didn't have much to say. She had dealt with all this for so long. The children took their treats and went to watch TV. Jill went with them.

"Jain, talk to me. Don't you know how much I care? I want to be a part of your life. Jamie wants to help too." He really was sincere and Jain knew it, but she just couldn't open up to him.

"I'm ok. It's been going on for so long, but it's almost over now. I don't understand it all, but I will. You know how the Bible says that there is nothing covered that won't be uncovered or something like that? Well, I think it's all going to come out now. I dread it for the kids' sake. They don't deserve this mess."

"No, they don't and neither do you. I'll be at court with you Monday. Jamie is going to take the kids for the day. We will meet you there. There is no need for the children to have to sit through that. You are not alone, Jain. There may be other church members there too." He put his arm around her shoulder and she wanted so very badly to just lean on him, but she didn't. She stood there stoically, almost holding her breath.

"Ok, I can take a hint, but I'll see you Monday." He stopped at the doorway and looked back. "Jain- -, he sighed, shook his head and went out. She heard him stop and say goodbye to the kids and Jill. She was still standing there when the sound of the motor faded away. He had said that she wasn't alone, but it sure did feel like it sometimes. Her emotions were in turmoil; she was upset and confused. One moment, she was glad that she would soon have closure after all these years, then she was mad at Ray and all the others that had caused her so much pain. She was so thankful that she had her children, family and friends, yet she still felt so alone. She knew that without God's help she would have given up. That was a sobering thought. What would the children do without her?

She rushed out the back door and into the wooded area behind the back yard. There was a big stump there and Jain went down on her knees and used it for an altar. The words poured from her heart and tears streamed from her eyes. At times she couldn't even say words, all she could do was groan. In anguish she asked God why he had done this to her and what had she ever done to deserve it. Then she was sorry and ashamed, for she knew that He hadn't done it. When she became aware of her surroundings once more, it was getting dark. Her knees were caked with dirt and dried pieces of bark stuck to her arms and clothing, but she felt much better. She stood and headed toward the house, where the kids had every single light on, even the porch lights. She entered the house to the sounds of the kids complaining that they were hungry and Jill wiggling in agreement. Jain realized that she was also hungry, starving was more like it. They ate a large meal, had their baths and went to bed. Jain lay there reading her Bible, still sorry that she had questioned God. Lord, do you understand? She wondered. She turned in her bed and lost the page that she was reading. When she started to turn the page back, she looked at the verse where her thumb lay. It was Mark15: 34, where Jesus had asked God "Why has Thou forsaken me?" She closed the Bible and went to sleep. Peace had returned.

Monday was a gloomy day. There was a fine mist of a rain falling. On the way to the courthouse, Jain had to keep turning the windshield wipers on and off. The kids were silent. She found a parking place and they went through the double doors and up the stairs to the courtroom. They were a little early; still there was already a crowd. People were talking and all their words seemed to run together so that you only heard a few words that were understood. As Jain and the kids made their way through the crowd in front of the courtroom doors, a hush fell around them. They held hands and kept their heads down until they were inside. Even inside, it seemed that everyone was staring at them as they stood looking for a place to sit. Someone came up from behind and placed their hands on Jain's shoulder. She jumped in spite of the fact that she could see Ray and Roni sitting right there in front of her.

"Sorry, I didn't mean to scare you."

"Brad!"

"Jamie!"

Her children said these words in unison. What was that she heard in their voices? Joy? Relief? She wasn't sure, but Jamie gathered a child on each side and bent down to talk to them. Brad kept his hands on her shoulders. She felt a little of her strength return.

People were beginning to come in behind them and Jain was jolted back to reality as she heard a woman say, “Who’s that good looking man standing there with Jain?”

“I don’t know, but she sure can pick the good looking ones.”

“Yes, but can she keep them?” The woman who had spoken first laughed and he friend joined in.

“Why would he want Jain when he could have that beautiful creature standing there beside him?” Asked her friend.

Jamie had stepped up and the children had huddled next to their mother. Jain’s face had turned red, but Jamie’s was white.

"Jamie, I - -" Jain had intended to tell Jamie that she would never do anything to cause her pain, but she didn't get the chance.

Jamie had moved between the women and Brad, Jain and the kids. She had both hands planted firmly on her hips. "What right do you have to talk about us that way?" she demanded. "You don't know Brad and you don't know me. Contrary to what some people think, we are not inbred and we don't marry our cousins!" You must not know Jain very well either, or you wouldn't say such things! Her fists were clenched.

She glanced back at Brad and her anger abated. A silent message passed between them. She smiled a little and looked down at her feet. Her face was now getting red while Jain's had gone white. Brad just stood there grinning. He was now messaging Jain's shoulders. Later, he would have to explain the hard times and the closeness that he and Jamie had endured in their childhood years.

Cass and Stan stood with awed expressions on their faces looking up at Jamie. The two women looked like they were in shock. Everyone else was quiet. Jamie took a slow, deep breath.

"I'm sorry," She smiled at the women, and the sweet, loving person that Jain knew from church was back. "I shouldn't have lost my temper like that, but you still have no right to treat Jain that way. Brad is a wonderful person, but even if he weren't my cousin, I wouldn't have a chance with him with the way that he feels about Jain. That should answer your question about her being able to keep him. If you ladies aren't busy next Sunday, I'd like to invite you to come to church. Come on kids, let's get going."

The children exchanged their mother's hands for Jamie's and the three of them swept from the room with their heads held high. Brad guided Jain to a seat. She looked up and straight into the hostile stares of Roni and Ray. Brad put his arm around her shoulder and smiled, first at Jain and then at them. Others arrived and sat down. The room was divided with Ray and Roni's friends on one side of the isle and others on the other side. A few people from church came in and would smile or place a hand on Jain's shoulder, then take a seat behind her. Lisa and Jim walked in hand in hand. They looked happy for the first time in ages. Roni squirmed and Ray held her hand. Jain saw Lydia and Ray's brothers come in and sit across the isle on the front row. Bill, Ray and a few other officers went to sit with them, leaving Roni and her lawyer sitting at a table in the little boxed in area in front of the judge's seat. Papers were spread in front of them.

When the judge arrived and everyone rose, Jain was surprised. She had expected it to be the local judge, but it was someone that no one knew. He wore his black robe and his hair was prematurely gray. He seamed serious about his job.

Ray and Roni looked like they were in a panic. Even the lawyers looked surprised. A news crew from Nashville was there. Jain began to notice that the courtroom was packed and a lot of the people were strangers. The judge sat down looked toward the door. A woman, escorted by a state trooper came in and the whole room gasped. She was almost the exact image of Jain! A few years older, a little gray in the temples, two or three inches taller and ten pounds heavier, if not for that, they could have been twins. They sat beside the man and his children in the front row. Ray's side of the room was already full. The woman smiled at Roni, but Roni didn't smile back.

The voices started as whispers and rose to a roar. "My God!" "Who is that?" "She looks just like Jain!" "Why did the police bring?"

"ORDER!" The judge banged his gavel. "Order in the court." The room grew quiet. Bulbs flashed as the news crew took pictures.

Brad's arm tightened on Jain's shoulder and she realized that she'd been holding her breath. She took a deep breath and looked around. Roni was looking at the woman with the same hatred that she had for Jain. Ray looked confused. Brenda came in late and sat down near Jain. She raised her eyebrows as if to say, "This should be interesting."

Court was called into session and the charges against Roni were read. Jain was in for another shock. Roni was charged with the murder of Molly Jets. Just for a moment, Jain didn't realize what was going on. She thought she had not heard right, then she heard the soft sobbing and saw the man in the front row put his arm around the kids that sat beside him. The woman from out of state! The one they thought was her! Jain had thought this trial was about Ray getting shot. Jake and Roni must have shot that woman.

It all made sense now, the no bail, Bill not being allowed to see Roni, the strict security. The fact that Roni was held in jail even though Ray said that he shot himself.

The judge threatened to clear the courtroom and people grew quiet. Jain realized that she was not the only one who was surprised. Most of them had thought that this trial was about what had happened to Ray. They all knew about those charges, but no one had expected this. Jain thought Ray and Bill were both going to pass out. Roni, the only one who wasn't in shock, entered a plea of not guilty. She actually smiled and batted her eyelashes at the judge, and he smiled back. Jain realized that her mouth was open and she closed it. Everyone in the room seemed to be in the same state of mind. Jain looked at the people in the jury box and was surprised to find that she didn't know any of them. Over half of them were women.

Opening statements were made. Jain had hardly recognized the DA as the same man she had met in his office. He was wearing a suit and he was all business. Gone was the gentle man who had smiled so kindly and made her feel at ease in his office. This man was a force to be reckoned with. He demanded respect and he got it. When he made his statement, saying that the state would prove beyond a doubt that Roni Davis was guilty of the murder of Molly Jets, the courtroom hung on his every word. He told them about the night that Molly died, how she was shot while driving her car down the highway. He told them about the two children in the car with her, how it was a miracle that they were not harmed, and about the witness' to the act. The shocker came when he told them that he would prove that Roni shot and killed Mrs. Jets thinking that she was killing Jain Davis. Everyone looked at Jain and at the Jets and at the woman who looked so much like Jain. The whispers started again and the judge banged his gavel. Roni, for once in her life, looked frightened. Ray was as pale as a ghost. Roni's lawyer asked for a recess.

The judge had the lawyers to approach the bench. Jain couldn't hear what was being said, but the discussion was heated. All three men looked angry. They shook their heads and clenched their fists. The conference seemed to last forever. Finally, the judge announced that court would adjourn and reconvene at nine in the morning. Jain sat there, unable to move. People started to leave the room. She was aware that Brad was once again messaging her shoulders. Ray seemed to be cemented to his seat. Bill sat beside him, but for once, he wasn't saying a word. Roni and her lawyer seemed to be arguing. The room was emptier now, much quieter, and Jain could hear some of the conversations.

"They have the gun and the bullet matches the one that they took from the Jets woman's car!" This came from Roni's lawyer. "They have a witness, for God's sake! You are going to have to change your plea to not guilty by reason of insanity if you have any chance of getting off. Look, Roni, if it was the local judge and the people in this town, it would be different, but we're not dealing with Bill and the local judge. These are people brought in by the FBI. This is serious stuff."

"I want another lawyer! If you can't get me off, I want someone who can!" Roni glared at her lawyer. "This is all Jain's fault. She should be the one locked up in jail."

"I've called in some other lawyers to help. They will be here tonight, but they are expensive. Can Ray come up with the money? They are the best in the state, but I don't think you are going to beat this."

"Just do something!" Roni said this over her shoulder as the policeman was leading her back to jail.

Everyone was gone now except for Jain, Brad, and Ray and Bill. Bill and Ray got up and left together. Both looked at Jain like they could kill her. She stood and would have fallen if Brad hadn't been holding onto her. She was having trouble understanding it all. Roni killed that woman thinking it was Jain, but who was the driver, who was helping her? Was it Jake? Had they really been trying to kill her for that long? Jake wasn't an amateur. He had been one of the top ten most wanted criminals in the United States. She remembered the dream of the man trying to shoot her and of her protector. It was awesome. It dawned on her that God was her protector and if not for him, she'd be dead and her children at the mercy of a cold, cruel world. They wouldn't even have a daddy to care for them. Her heart broke for Mr. Jets and his two children. Brad had walked her out of the courtroom and she wasn't even aware of it. News vans were everywhere. Reporters were snapping her picture and asking her questions. She ignored them and Brad tried to shield her from them. Jain was glad that Jamie had the kids away from all this. When the D.A. appeared on the courthouse steps, and the reporters mobbed him, Brad rushed her to his car and drove away. He went in the opposite direction for a few miles and took the back roads around town and back to her house so that they wouldn't be followed. She hadn't said a word, and was barely aware that Brad kept glancing at her.

Chapter12

Jain was at the courthouse every day, and Brad was with her. Jamie practically moved in with the kids. Lucy was also camped out at Jain's house. Roni's lawyer had made his opening statement on Tuesday, and asked for a little more time for his co-council to arrive.

The trial made the news every day. Flash bulbs went off each time they entered or left the courthouse. Jain was surprised that they didn't invade her home. She heard that they were watching Ray's house. They interviewed Roni and her family. They interviewed Bill, who told them that it was all just a big mistake. When they cut the interview off, he was still saying, "Why, that girl wouldn't hurt anyone! This is just ridiculous…" The chief of police called him into the office and told him that if he wanted to keep his job, he would keep his mouth shut. Bill was somber after that and Jain actually found herself feeling sorry for him. Brad thought it was funny. Lisa said that Bill was beyond crazy and they must just let him be a cop because they felt sorry for him. Jamie said very little, and Lucy went around shaking her head and saying, "I just can't believe this! I really can't."

Roni seemed to be holding up well. She wore her make up and her best cloths. Her skirts and pants were a little tight and her necklines were a little low cut, but gone were the cut off jean shorts with raveled legs and her buttocks hanging out. Once in a while, she would let those huge, crocodile tears flow from her huge blue eyes. Lisa would moan and say; "Oh no, here she goes again! Look Jain, look. See Roni cry!" Jain knew that Lisa would never get over being fooled by Roni's tears. Roni's lawyers were very attentive. They had numerous assistants, coming and going at a rapid pace. It was almost like Roni was a queen holding court. On Wednesday, Roni had two lawyers sitting in the little boxed in area with her. The new lawyer looked very impressive, very expensive, but the DA wasn't intimidated. Jain saw the Judge glance at him before asking if he was ready to continue.

The DA looked up from scribbling on his pad. "Yes, Your Honor,"

Mr. Jets was called to the stand. He was sworn in and took his seat in the witness chair beside the judge. He stated his name and with tears rolling down his cheeks he explained what had happened to his wife. She and the children had been to a family reunion in Fairview and were traveling through Hohenwald on their way home to Alabama. He had been unable to go with them because he had to work, but Molly and the kids went anyway because she hadn't seen her family in over six months. Her aunt and a cousin that she had not seen in three years were going to be there. They had only stayed for two days and were driving home late because they wanted to get home and have the family back together. Mr. Jets sobbed as he told the story. He had talked to his wife on the phone just an hour before she left. He had tried to get her to take the interstate, but she wouldn't. She was taking the shortest route home. His oldest child, a daughter had told him the rest after they buried Molly.

They were going south on highway 48 and were about five miles out of town, when the kids started fussing and saying they were hungry. Molly knew the roads and that it was a long way before she would be able to find a store that was open. She decided to go back to town and get food to keep the kids happy while she drove home. She turned around and started back. That's when the big truck came up behind her. It kept getting closer and closer. At first she thought the driver was angry, that maybe she had pulled out in front of him without seeing him. She slowed and moved closer to the right side of the road to let him pass, but he just kept riding her bumper. He tried to force her off the road, but she was afraid to stop. When they reached the top of the hill and started down, he hit her from behind. She fought for control and almost got the car back on the road, but that's when they shot her and the car went off the side of the hill. The kids were scared and were holding onto each other in the back seat, afraid to move or speak, until they heard the gunshots. That's when they started screaming.

All of this and more came out despite the many objections of Roni's lawyers. The children sobbed softly as their dad told the story. The gun was entered into evidence. They also had the bullet, which had been remover from Molly's brain and the one that had been removed from Ray. They proved that both were fired from the same gun. The defense argued that Jake had shot Ray, and that it was Possible that Jake had also been the one that shot and killed Molly.

The eighteen-year-old girl and the twenty-year-old boy that had witnessed the crime were called to the stand. They testified that the man was driving and that a blond woman had fired the gun. The girl identified Roni as the shooter. Roni's finger prints were still on the gun, though not as plain as Jake's. A description of Molly's car and of Jain's was given and a picture of each car was entered into evidence. They were almost identical. Witnesses were called to tell of the hostile relationship between Roni and Jain. Mrs. Hunter's report was entered into evidence. The defense had wanted it there and the state had no objection. The restraining orders that until now, had only been a waste of Jain's time were entered into evidence. The DA had wanted that.

The spectators in the courtroom were quiet now. It was a completely different atmosphere. You wouldn't believe that they were the same crowd. Roni's lawyers were often red faced as they talked quietly but earnestly with her. They gestured with their hands. Roni remained stoic, determined to be found not guilty. Ray looked like he'd been dead and drug off for a week and Bill wasn't doing much better. Jim was doing very well. He was seldom present, and when he was there, Lisa was by his side. They were back together. Roni's supporters had dwindled. They were now mostly curious, about Roni, not Jain. They almost forgot Jain.

Jain began to hope that she would not have to testify, but her hopes were dashed on Friday. The children were back to an almost normal routine. They left early Friday morning to spend the weekend with Brenda. It was raining again. Jain felt sad and alone. It seemed like the world was crying, as she dressed and left the house. She felt like crying, but didn't know why.

She drove to the courthouse alone, and slipped into a seat in the back. She saw the DA look the room over and felt his eyes come to rest on her. He smiled to himself, but tried to hide it by looking down and scribbling on his pad. Roni's lawyers were not smiling. The judge entered and they all rose. Court was called to order and the DA was instructed to call his first witness.

"The state calls Jain Davis to the stand."

For a moment, she couldn't breath. Her knees were weak when she stood and slowly made her way to the stand. She was shaking inside and feared that it showed on the outside. She was solemn as she placed her hand on the Bible and swore to tell the truth. She silently prayed for the strength to get through it. The DA maneuvered between her and the defense table and somehow he was also able to block the view between Jain and the judge. When he was sure that he had her attention, he smiled at her and then he winked! Jain was shocked, but it worked. She began to relax a little. He moved back to his normal place and now appeared very serious.

"Please state your name, address and occupation for the court."

Jain did as she was asked and was surprised that her voice sounded normal.

"Mrs. Davis, do you live approximately one mile from the place where Molly Jets died?"

"Yes"

"Do you travel this road often?"

"Almost every day, going to and from work."

"You stated that you are a nurse and that you work at the local hospital. What shift do you work? What are your working hours?"

Jain stammered. "Uh, I work different hours, sometimes I work days, but I work a lot of evening shifts and even some midnights. We're often short staffed."

"Would you please tell the court what is your relationship to Ray Davis?"

"He is my ex-husband, the father of my children."

"Prior to the time that your marriage fell apart, did you know the defendant, Roni Davis?"

"No."

"Since the divorce, has Roni Davis continuously harassed you and your children?"

"Yes."

"Objection!" Both of Roni's lawyers were on their feet.

"Sustained!" The judge looked angry.

The DA looked down, "Sorry Your Honor, that's all the questions I have for Mrs. Davis. If there is no cross, I call June Morlon to the stand."

Jain stepped down and the lawyer was somehow in front of her again, slowing her progress. The woman who looked so much like Jain was making her way to the stand. He moved aside and Jain and June were standing about two feet apart. The jury and the people in the courtroom gasped. Jain proceeded to her seat and June took the stand.

When June was sworn in, everyone was once again shocked, for even their voices were similar. June looked at Roni with sadness in her eyes, but Roni glared back with hatred.

The DA hesitated a moment for this to be noticed, then he asked; "Mrs. Morlon, what is your relationship to Roni Davis?"

"Roni is my niece."

"Is it a good relationship? Are you close?"

"We used to be, when she was little, but no, not anymore." She looked ready to cry as she glanced at Roni.

Roni looked like she would explode at any moment. The defense lawyers were on their feet objecting. The lawyers all approached the bench and the DA explained that he was going to show that Roni's relationship with her aunt was directly related to her relationship with Jain and that the similarities of Molly and Jain all contributed to Molly's death. He had an eight by ten picture of Molly in his hand that he managed to hold where it could be seen by everyone at one time or another. They argued for a long time and everyone was angry, even the judge. The rest of the courtroom was hushed. It ended with the photo being admitted as evidence and the witness being excused, but the DA did get the right to recall her at a later time if he chose to do so.

The evidence against Roni continued to grow. The atmosphere in the courtroom was different now. Roni was now the focus of everyone's attention instead of Jain. The DA took two weeks and two days to present his case. Jain was surprised that Jake was not really the focus of the case, only that Roni was with him when she shot and killed Molly, thinking that she was killing Jain. The talk around town was that Roni was guilty. Everyone thought so, except Bill. Ray sold his house and moved in with his mother to pay Roni's attorneys. He lost his job from missing so much work. Lydia blamed it all on Jain, and so did Ray, but no threats were made. No one damaged her home or wrote nasty notes and left them in her mailbox. Jain slept poorly some nights, but the warning dreams had stopped. The trial still made the news, but not as often. Jain found out over the news that Jake was now on Death's Row in Texas. June was still escorted to court every day by the police, but she was not confined in jail. She was staying with Roni's grandmother. Ray continued to be in court every day and to look longingly at Roni, but she just ignored him. The DA told Jain that she didn't really have to be there now, but that he really wanted her to be. He said that it was good for his case, though he thought that the evidence alone would get a conviction. He even convinced her to come in late dressed in her uniform a few times and to go from the courtroom to work. Jain had agreed to work evening shift until the trial concluded. She still had a lot of unanswered questions. By now, Jain realized that this guy was good at his job! Roni had definitely met her match. She wasn't so sure, though, on the day Roni's defense really got started. As soon as the judge was seated, the lawyers approached the bench.

They argued quietly, but desperately, for about ten minutes. An agreement was finally reached and the DA shook his head, threw up his hands and walked over to his seat and sat down. There he pouted like a small child would do and made no attempt to hide it. It was announced for the record that the defendant had changed her plea from not guilty to one of not guilty by reason of insanity. A murmur was heard through out the room and the judge banged his gavel. The crowed silenced and Roni's lawyers called their first witness. It was June Morlon and Roni did her best to act subdued.

June testified that when Roni was thirteen years old, she came to Texas and lived with her and Jake for a little over two years. Roni's family had come out for a two-week visit on their vacation. They had been having a lot of trouble with Roni. Her grades were failing. She was skipping school and running with a crowd of older children, mostly boys. She seemed to hate her parents, always yelling and talking back to them. They had forced her to come to get her away from that group that she hung out with and she was very angry. June had tried to bond with her, help out a little, but with no luck. Jake, however, was a different story. Roni stuck to him like a shadow, and this seemed to delight him. June was surprised, because Jake had never wanted children. Their marriage had a lot of problems, so June entertained her sister and her brother in law while Roni tagged along with Jake. When the visit was over, Roni announced that she was staying. Jake said that it sounded good to him, and it made no difference what the rest of them said. Without her sister around, June soon realized she had a world of problems. Roni and Jake ran the house and ignored her, except to tell her to cook food, clean house, etc. She confronted Jake about the situation and he beat her until she could not get up. Roni sat on the stairs and watched it all. June was concerned about what this would do to her, but when she looked at her face, Roni was smiling. Jake, who was standing over her, followed her gaze and said, 'come on Sugar Pie, I guess we're eating out tonight.' Roni had bounded down the steps to his side. Jake put his arm around her shoulders and hugged her, but Roni threw both arms around his neck and kissed him hard in the mouth. June had crawled over to the phone and was calling the police. Jake noticed before she completed the last number and slammed the receiver down, crushing her hand with his. She held up her right hand and you could see that the bones were crooked. He told her that if she ever tried that again, he would kill her, and she had believed him. Roni and Jake didn't come home that night. June crawled to the sofa and slept there.

When people questioned her about her bruises the next day, she told them that she had fallen down the stairs. When Jake and Roni did come home, they acted as if everything was just fine.

Jake started taking Roni to the firing range and teaching her to shoot. She loved it. One day, Jake called June to come and pick them up. He said the car wouldn't start. When she got there, they were not in the car, so she went inside to look for them. She found them and knew that Jake had meant for her to do so. He was standing behind Roni with his arms around her waist. When he looked back and saw June, he slid his hands up and cupped Roni's breast. He whispered something in her ear, and they both laughed. They walked over, arms around each other, and told her that she wasn't needed after all, the car was working just fine now. When they came home two days later, June tried to talk to Roni. She had called Roni's parents, but that had ended with them all mad and not speaking to each other for the last few years. She also tried to talk to Jake, but he just laughed at her. She had packed her cloths and left, but Jake found her and brought her back. He had tied her to the bed and with his knife, he carved his name in her belly while she screamed and Roni watched in fascination. He told her that if she ever left again, he would cut a lot deeper and make her hurt a lot more.

The DA had objected to all of this, but the defense had convinced the Judge that it was necessary to their case. They called in an expert to testify how all this had affected Roni. He said that Roni was angry with her aunt for not protecting her from all this and that she had transferred all these emotions to Jain. The people were all focused on Roni and all this new information now and Jain felt less stress. She looked around at all the different emotions playing on the faces around her. She was absolutely fascinated by the many and vivid expressions on the DA's face. He would shake his head, clench his fist, and at times, he would almost rise out of his seat. Jain thought again that he had missed his calling. He even looked good enough to be an actor. 'What else have I missed?' she wondered, 'caught up in my own little world of horrors. With the pressure off, she was seeing things that surprised her. She found herself smiling more often these days, but when she looked at Ray, she couldn't smile. He was loosing weight. He never smiled. He almost begged for a kind word or look form Roni.

Roni's attorneys looked worried, even Roni was somber and managed a few tears once in awhile. When she did this, the DA rolled his eyes and looked toward the ceiling. He watched the response of everyone in the room. Jain got to the point where she could feel when his eyes were resting on her. She was so afraid that she might get called back to the stand, and so relieved when she didn't.

They put Roni on the stand and she let those huge, giant teardrops fall from her big blue eyes. Now Lisa was making as many faces as the DA, and squirming in her seat. To Jain's surprise, Roni admitted that she shot Molly.

With tears rolling down her cheeks, she cried, "I thought it was Jain! It's her that should be dead!" She told how she was only sixteen when she got involved with Ray. She said that Jain just wouldn't let go and let them be happy. She accused Jain of using her kids to get to Ray. She ranted and raved about how horrible Jain was. Then she blurted out that Jake was the only one who would help her, the only one who had ever understood her. When her lawyers led her from the stand, she was pointing at Jain, screaming," It's all her fault, Your Honor, if you will just listen to me, I can get this all straightened out!" The gavel was banging again. The judge was calling for order and threatening to throw people in jail. The DA was smiling.

Ray tried to get to Roni to comfort her, but two uniformed policemen escorted him back to his seat and told him that if he didn't control himself, he would have to vacate the courtroom. Everyone was talking. The judge was once again banging his gavel and saying, "ORDER!" Finally, court was dismissed. Closing statements would start tomorrow. Jain slipped out and went home.

She had thought that she would be upset over the day's events, but she wasn't. She ate supper, unplugged the phone, locked the doors, and went to bed and slept like a baby. The next morning, she overslept and had a quick cup of coffee while she dressed and hurried to her car. She hesitated when she saw the envelope under her windshield wiper. She opened it and read:

> *Didn't get an answer when I called you or your sister, so I drove out to see about you. Jill was happy and the door was locked so I figured you were exhausted and sleeping. I have tomorrow off and will see you there.*
>
> *Love, Brad*

Jain smiled, then wondered why he didn't have to work. He was waiting for her on the steps. Jain felt someone's eyes on her and saw the DA watching as Brad slipped his arm around her waist. She half expected him to come over and tell her to look heartbroken over Ray or something, but he just waved and went inside. When court was in session, he made his closing statement, no faces and no gestures. He was very serious. He paced slowly in front of the jury and in the front of the room and picked up evidence from time to time. He didn't have his notepad. He wore his very expensive suit and tie. He seemed to look everyone directly in the eye. If he had said that the sky was red instead of blue, it would have been hard not to believe it.

"Ladies and gentlemen, don't be deceived by all the antics and theatrics that you have seen in this trial. The state has proved beyond a doubt that Roni Davis is guilty of murder. By her own admission, she shot and killed Molly as she drove down the road with her two children in the car with her. It was by the grace of God that the children were not harmed. We have the physical evidence. We have the gun, Roni's prints on the gun. We have the bullet that was removed from Molly's head. We have proof that the bullet came from Roni's gun. We have eyewitnesses to the crime. We have linked Roni to the serial killer, Jake Morlon, who is now awaiting execution in Texas. He was with her in the truck when she committed the murder. We have proof that they attempted to murder Roni's husband, Ray Davis. Although we didn't' go into it in great detail, we have proof that Roni threatened the life of Jain Davis and her children. She's a murderer, ladies and gentlemen. Don't be fooled by her ability to act. This woman, whom the defense is trying to pass off as a girl, is a heartless killer who shot and killed in cold blood, robbing a man of his beloved wife and two innocent children of their mother. She knew what she wanted and she knew what she was doing. That is all that mattered to her. That she shot the wrong woman doesn't make it any less murder. She stated that she thought that she was killing Jain Davis. Had she succeeded, she would have left two children orphans. Yes, I said orphans. You see their biological father sitting here in the courtroom, but he walked away and left them years ago, let them for Roni." He shook his head and cleared his throat. He took a moment to look earnestly into the eyes of the jurors again.

"Folks, this is a woman with no conscious. You cannot let her go. The defense is going to try to tell you that she was insane, that she didn't know what she was doing, that Jain drove her to it. Just remember folks, that it was Roni who took Jain's husband, not the other way around, and she still wanted Jain dead. The defense is going to tell you about Roni's problems with her parents when she was a rebellious teenager and use this to say she was not responsible for what she did, but it won't wash. Lots of teens have problems with their parents. They don't go out and kill people. Remember, Roni is no longer a teenager. She is an adult now and has been one for several years. She is well beyond the age of accountability! Even if she were still a teen, they can be tried as adults for crimes such as this. She is guilty. She is a cold, heartless murder! If you set her free, she will do it again. We ask that you find her guilty and we seek the death penalty."

Jain heard the sigh from everyone in the building and she heard the now familiar sound of the judge banging the gavel. Then there was nothing but quiet. One of the defense attorneys stood up, opened his mouth, turned around, and then sat back down without a word. The judge banged his gavel again and said, "Court will reconvene in the morning at nine am. I want all council in my chambers. NOW!"

Everyone cleared out, except for Ray and Bill, who sat on the front row watching them half lead and half drag Roni out, and Jain and Brad in the back of the building. All were stunned except for Brad, who gently squeezed Jain's hand. He pulled her to her feet and led her outside.

"Honey, I have an appointment that I have to keep. It won't take over twenty minutes or so. If you can wait, I'll take you to lunch."

Still numb, she sat on the top step and nodded. "I think I need a few minutes to myself anyway. Go ahead and do what you need to. If I'm not here when you get back, I'll be across the street at the grocery store."

Jain propped her elbows on her knees and sat trying to clear her mind. She really believed now, that Roni would be convicted. Ray! What would he do? Would he just give up? Would he blame Jain? Oh yes! She knew he'd do that. Would it all start over again? Could Roni really get the death penalty? She knew that Jake was going to be electrocuted. What would all this do to her children? She took a deep breath as reality hit her hard. At the same time she heard whistling and the DA burst through the door.

"Jain." Want to go get some lunch? I believe I've won this case and I've been living in this town exactly seven years to day."

She stood. "I - -Uh- -No, I'm waiting for Brad. Thanks." What was this? She seemed to become a blubbering idiot in the presence of this man.

"Hmm, You know, Jain, I've watched you over the last few years. I've seen you help a lot of folks since you became a nurse. You're a good person. I think things are going to get better for you. Now tell me, could a guy ask you out to dinner sometime, or is it really serious with that guy that hovers over you so much?"

"Brad. I'm waiting for him to get back."

"Yeah, you said that." He smiled at her. "This thing is gonna end tomorrow, Jain. Be sure to be here." He kissed her quickly on the cheek and headed jauntily on toward his office across the street. He waved at Brad as his car turned into the parking lot, but Brad didn't wave back. Jain knew from the look on Brad's face that he had seen that peck on the cheek. He must have very good vision. Actually, she knew he'd been looking to see if she was still at the courthouse or at the grocery store, but when he got out the car, she said: "Hello Superman. How's the x-ray vision?"

He laughed. "Hey there, Lois. Let's go eat lunch." He planted his kiss on her lips and she didn't know or care if anyone was looking. She held onto him. In the restaurant, they were more quiet. Both were kind of lost in their own thoughts.

"It's really going to end tomorrow. The trial will be over." Jain sipped her tea.

"It's almost like it is already over. Roni is going to have to pay. I mean, what can her lawyers say? It was all summed up today. He covered his evidence and theirs too, and he did a very good job. Let's go get the kids and Jill and go play on the banks of the Tennessee River for awhile. We can be there in less than an hour and stay until dark. Let's forget the trial for awhile."

Chapter 13

They were all at court the next morning before nine am. The children had come even though Jain didn't want them to. She told herself that they had a right to be there and it might make Ray feel better. She didn't know that the reason that they wanted to be there was to support their Mom. They ignored Ray and clung close to Jain's side. Jamie stuck just as close to Brad. Brenda was there and Lucy had even dragged Frank along with her. Lisa joined the group with Jim in tow and said: "Oh! I wouldn't miss this for the world!"

The news crews were back. The room was so crowded that people were standing along the back wall. Jain had a feeling that they were disappointed. Roni's lawyer got up to give his closing statement. It lasted about thirty minutes. He could say nothing that had not been said before and when he tried to place the blame for Roni's actions on everyone else, he found no sympathy. He blamed Roni's family for exposing her to the likes of Jake Morlon and he blamed Jain for the problems in Roni's marriage. He said that Roni had killed Molly Jets thinking that Molly was Jain and that she only wanted to kill Jain because she was driven to it. He pounded his fist and proclaimed that Roni was no threat to society. He concluded by saying that Roni needed help and possibly hospitalization, not prison and certainly not the death penalty. Roni was quiet as she hung on every word.

Almost everyone hung around the courthouse for hours, waiting to see if the jury would reach a verdict. The lawyers came and went. Brenda took the kids to eat, promising that she'd have them back before the jury returned. Jain saw the DA stop and give an interview to the news crews. After they were satisfied and lost interest in him, he called Jain off for a talk. Jamie gave him a stern look and stepped closer to Brad, who wrapped his arm over her shoulder. Knowing how worried Jain was, Brad ruffled her hair and said: "Don't forget about the x-ray vision. You'll be fine." He gave her a gentle push toward the DA.

They went into his office and he had her sit in the same chair that she had sat in the first time they met. He sat on the edge of his desk and laughed. "Relax Jain. It's all over but the crying. I think Roni's tears are going to be real now. I just wanted to thank you for all your help. Your presence in that courtroom was a lot of help to this case. The jury liked you. Listen, it's pretty obvious that you and that guy Brad are an item, but we're friends aren't we? What do you say to introducing me to that gorgeous creature that's always hovering over him?"

Jain laughed out loud. "Be careful what you say to Jamie about her relationship with Brad. I've watched you during this trial and I was very impressed. I thought that you missed your calling and that maybe you should have been an actor, but Jamie can handle you. You mentioned lunch the other day, come on, let's go see if we can feed Jamie and Brad." She was still laughing and leading him by the hand, when she walked up to Jamie.

"Jamie, meet Mr. James K. Wilterman, the district attorney of Lewis county. He wants to buy you lunch and I think Brad and I should come along with you. I'm starving." She noticed that Jamie was speechless, so she punched the DA on the arm and said: "Feed her some blueberry pie."

As they were finishing lunch, James got a call that the jury was coming in and they rushed back. The news coverage was also back. Camera bulbs flashed and reporters called their names as they made their way to the courtroom. Once again, it was filled to capacity. Everyone was solemn. It was almost as if everyone was holding their breath.

Roni sat haunched over the table biting her nails. The bailiff said "All rise" and the judge entered and told them to be seated. Jain looked at everyone. She caught herself holding her breath as Brad held her hand. Ray sat by Bill and they both looked like they would pass out at any moment. Mr. Jets sat up front and held his children close. You could have heard a pin drop.

"Mr. foreman, have you reached a verdict?" The judge's voice carried well.

"We have, your honor."

A piece of folded paper was carried to the judge. He looked at and nodded.

"What is your verdict"

"We find the defendant guilty. We recommend life in prison."

Roni jumped up, screaming "NO! You can't do this."

Her lawyers tried to calm her. Ray got to his feet and tried to get to her, but he buckled and went down on his knees. Bill sat like a statue. Roni's supporters were quiet. Lisa and a few others seemed to be having a party in the back. People were talking to the reporters. Jain's first rational thought was to get the kids out of there.

"Come on, we need to go." She took a child by each hand and gently pulled. "We will stop and let you say something to your dad and go home."

They stopped by Ray who was now sitting in a seat by the isle. Jain opened her mouth but no words came out.

"We're sorry for your loss, Ray." This came from Cass, but Jain heard echoes of herself. It was as if she were trying to comfort a stranger.

"Yeah, we're sorry." Mumbled Stan.

Now they were pulling on Jain's arms, urging her out the door. Ray didn't acknowledge them. He just sat there with his head in his hands and cried. There was nothing else to say or do. The lawyers took Roni away talking to her about trying to get an appeal. People were leaving.

Jain took the children home. They could be there before their friends realized that they were gone. They needed some time to themselves.

The news summed up the trial. Roni was sentenced to life in prison. It was not likely that she could appeal. There was talk of her standing trial for some things that had happened when she lived in Texas. Ray was quoted as saying that he would stand by her. Bill was quoted as saying that they had made a terrible mistake, Roni was innocent. Brad gave her a few days to herself. Things were too quiet. No nasty notes. No scary phone calls. No people looking at her and whispering. Jain slowly started to relax.

The next morning, she was awakened by laughter and noise out in the front yard. When she pulled on her robe and went out of her bedroom, she was greeted by the smell of fresh brewed coffee and she saw the take out food sitting on the table. She opened the front door to see Stan pitch the ball, Brad hit it, and Jill catch it. Cass was calling, "here Jill, here." between fits of laughter while standing on first base. Jain sat on the step and watched until Brad noticed that she was there.

"Game's over, kids." He went to the car, got something, then went to Jain. The kids and Jill gathered around. Brad got down on one knee and the kids giggled. Jain started to get up and he grabbed her hand.

"Jain, will you marry me?"

She couldn't get up now. She was suddenly made of rubber. She also couldn't speak, not even stammer. She nodded her head. Brad let out a whoop, grabbed her up in his arms and spun around. "She said yes!" The kids joined in the whooping and dancing. When he put her down, Brad slipped a beautiful ring on her finger. News of the engagement soon spread like wildfire. Jain was so happy.

This time, there was a church wedding. Stan carried the ring. Cass stood by her mother holding the bouquet. Jamie stood beside Jain. James Wilkerson was Brad's best man and so it seemed, his new best friend. Jamie and James were now inseparable. The building was packed. No one was crying. There were only smiles and nervous giggles. The children were going with them on the honeymoon. For just a moment, memories of her first marriage crept into Jain's mind, but she pushed them away. She realized that this 'Nothing and Nobody' was now exactly what she wanted to be.

About the Auhtor

Joyce Dicus is a registered nurse and the mother of two children. She has lived most of her life in a small town in Tennessee and loves it. It has been her lifelong dream to be an author. This is her first novel and is fiction, loosely based on the things that she has seen and experienced. She is passionate about her God, her family, and her job. She loves people who overcome obstacles and never give up.

Printed in the United States
932000005B